THE STEPDAUGHTERS

ROD WALEMAN

OPHELIA PRESS BOOKS, #627

1

THE STEPDAUGHTERS

ROD WALEMAN

COPYRIGHT 1971

THIS EDITION COPYRIGHT 2006 OLYMPIA PRESS.COM

ISBN: 1-59654-370-1

THE OPHELIA PRESS
AN IMPRINT OF DISRUPTIVE PUBLISHING, INC.

INTRODUCTION

"Women can adjust to anything," Petronius wrote in his *Satyricon* almost two thousand years ago, "so long as there is a man and a healthy penis involved." Petronius was referring to Roman women of his era, but he undoubtedly included *all* women of all times in his statement. He could not be unaware of the legendary history of Romulus and his soldiers who raped the Sabine virgins and carried them away as wives, for when the time came for the liberation of the females they refused to leave their virile captors. They had adjusted.

It is on this theme of adjustment that *Dansk Blue Books's* Rod Waleman has based his new novel, *The Stepdaughters.* Although it is, in essence, the story of the love-starved, widowed Valerie, we cannot ignore the presence of her two beautiful teenage daughters, Ethel and Penny, both of whom are in heated competition with mother for the attentions of Valerie's new husband, Mark.

Mr. Waleman's deft characterizations of the three passionate females, and of the smoothly functioning Mark, places his book far above the ordinary novel. His characters speak and move with authenticity and realism, and the action is so fast-paced that it is difficult to lay the book down once one has begun reading it. When we first meet Valerie Walker, we cannot help but feel her love, her trust, and a little of her incredulity that such a wonderfully virile man as Mark would be attracted to a widow with two daughters. We watch as she succumbs completely to his forceful personality and his animal vitality in bed. Then, coldly, Mark puts into operation his plan for complete domination of the household. The willowy, headstrong Ethel—at first teasingly and then with deadly seriousness—plays with Mark's proffered forbidden fire; instead of being burnt, she discovers she has received new and frighteningly potent

3

powers. The trusting, affectionate Penny is the next to find herself caught in Mark's web of sensual intrigue, and it is not until her childlike body is joyfully screaming out its ecstatic defiance to morality that she discovers she has become a woman.

When Mark's son by his first marriage, Neal, is brought to live in the household, Valerie realizes what is happening. It almost immediately becomes evident that Neal has some of his father's characteristics and attributes. Valerie, herself, fighting valiantly against her own hot, dark desires, is one of the first victims of Neal's strength and charm.

In time, Valerie is forced to adjust to this communal love setup. She must adjust ... or lose forever her husband and her happiness. It is at that moment she realizes, with horror, that this will be only the first of many adjustments she must make in the future. But can she adjust? Will she adjust to this immoral situation?

It would not be fair to the reader to reveal any more of this exciting story, for the ending itself is a classic, with the final sentence in the book being, "That was really the only thing that mattered." It is a denouement worthy of Balzac, Flaubert, Tolstoi, or Hemingway.

It is possible that the graphic scenes, explicit language, and sexual candor of the characters will offend some readers. But people like the Walker family *do* exist, and to deny them their day in this *Dansk Blue Book* court of public judgment is merely turning one's back on reality.

This is the story of survival—a survival of the species on one level, the survival of the fittest on a deeper level, and on the deepest level of all ... the survival of the need of physical love which was common to Adam and Eve and thus transcends all other hungers and needs.

We are grateful to Mr. Waleman for writing this novel. If you like *The Stepdaughters,* we know you will also

4

enjoy his first novel for *Dansk Blue Books, The Young Librarian.*

The Publishers North Hollywood, Cal. February, 1971

CHAPTER I

Valerie Walker applied a frosty-pale lipstick carefully before the bathroom mirror. She had the motel suite to herself for the moment since her daughters, Ethel and Penny, were off on some errand of their own and her husband, Mark, had had an early business appointment. Valerie had indulged herself by sleeping an extra hour.

The mirror in the bathroom between the two bedrooms reflected a tall, ash-blond, fresh-faced, full-bosomed woman with light blue eyes and marvelously clear skin. She put the lipstick away and smoothed her skirt over hips that flared spectacularly from her slender waist. Her woman friends were envious of her girlish waist and calves which emphasized the firm, matronly curves of her breasts and buttocks.

Satisfied with her appearance, she left the motel suite and went down the long corridor to the coffee shop. Her freshly lipsticked mouth broke into a wide smile when Mark stood up at a corner table and waved to her. She hurried to him and kissed his cheek lightly before taking the seat across from him. "Good morning, dear," she said warmly. "I'd have come sooner if I'd known your appointment was going to be a short one."

"Didn't know it myself," he said cheerfully as the waitress filled Valerie's coffee cup. Mark Walker was a handsome man, six-two, two hundred trim pounds, with black hair and a small mustache. He wore clothes well and had a debonair manner that suggested sophisticated tastes.

Valerie glanced around the coffee shop as she lifted her coffee cup to her lips. "Where are the girls, Mark?"

"I gave them money to do a little shopping," he replied.

"You're spoiling them outrageously!" Valerie protested.

"Nonsense, Val," he said briskly. Then he smiled. "And anyway, why shouldn't I spoil all three of my girls?"

Valerie felt a tide of color sweeping into her face at the look in Mark's eyes. She had been married to Mark Walker for only four months, the most thrilling months of her life. Ethel, almost seventeen, and Penny, almost sixteen, were her daughters by a marriage that had ended in widowhood for her eight years previously. She had never expected to be as happy as she found herself to be in the arms of Mark Walker, and she still found it exciting to wake mornings and rediscover his dark head on the next pillow. And best of all, the girls had taken to him almost immediately.

"Orange juice?" Mark suggested. "Eggs over with sausage?"

Valerie refused the orange juice but said yes to the eggs and sausage. She still had a little-girl feeling of well-being at Mark's casual inclusion of his whole new family on his business trips. Mark was an insurance broker and a prosperous one. They had moved into his handsome home around which Valerie was still feeling her way, and the feeling of money being available for luxuries still caused her to feel a bit giddy. And the girls loved it, of course.

Thinking of her daughters reminded Valerie of a point she wanted to bring up with Mark. She set down her coffee cup before speaking. "I'd like to make a suggestion," she began. "You don't have to decide right this minute, but I'd like you to be thinking about it. It's about your son, Neal." Valerie was Mark's third wife, and Neal, seventeen, was the son of his first marriage. Because Mark's second wife hadn't wanted the boy around the house he had spent his teenage years in a military academy.

"What would you think about bringing Neal home from the academy and letting him finish his last semester at the local high school with the girls?" Valerie continued. "He was really cute with them when he was home for a visit

8

three weeks ago, and I hated to see him go back to that place. He's had so little family life, Mark, and I get the feeling he's lonely. He's shy, but he has delightful manners." She leaned across the table slightly. "You've made me so happy, dear," she said softly, "I can't bear to think of anyone connected with us not being as happy as possible."

Mark was staring into the depths of his coffee cup. "Do you think the girls would adapt well to what would be an invasion of their private preserve?" he asked.

"I'm sure of it," Valerie said firmly. "Penny thought he was the greatest thing since her last roller coaster ride."

Mark smiled. "We'll think about it, then," he said. "You know you have two very nice daughters, Val. I had a cup of coffee with them this morning while they were breakfasting, and I asked them—quite seriously, I may add—" He smiled at her again. "If they felt I was making you properly happy. Ethel said promptly that anyone had only to look at you to know I was. Before I thought I said people should see us when we were alone t o g e t h e r." The smile quirked the corners of his attractive mouth.

"Fortunately the semi-suggestive nature of my response seemed to pass over their attractive young heads."

Valerie smiled, too. "Youngsters know so much more these days than we did when I was a girl, but I guess they don't know it all yet despite their pretensions to sophistication." Her eggs and sausage arrived, and she ate hungrily, accepting another cup of coffee from the waitress.

Mark leaned across the table as Valerie had previously. "You didn't ask me why I gave the girls shopping money," he said in an undertone. Valerie shook her head negatively, her mouth full of toast. "I couldn't give them money for the movies in the morning," Mark continued with a twinkle in his eye, "but I thought if I removed them from the vicinity of the suite, it just might be possible for me—" He leaned still closer and his voice lowered again.

9

"To persuade my wife to come back to our bedroom with me for a good fuck."

Valerie's cheeks pinkened but her eyes shone. Mark's ardency was a continuing revelation to her. Sex-starved for the years of her widowhood, she doubly appreciated this virile man who could melt her with a glance. "Your wife is very easy to persuade, sir," she replied demurely. Under cover, of the table she reached across and gave Mark's thigh a quick squeeze.

"More coffee?" he asked as she finished her eggs.

She shook her head as she rose from the table. Picking up her handbag, she walked around the table and placed her lips against Mark's ear. "I'd rather have the fuck," she murmured.

He laughed aloud, and heads turned in their direction. Valerie's color heightened again at the attraction she had drawn by causing Mark's masculine guffaw, but she was proud of the appearance she knew they made. His big hand had already started in the direction of her hips before he remembered their public position, and the hand fell to his side.

Mark paid the bill and they returned along the corridor to the suite, Valerie walking a bit faster than usual. Inside, she locked the door, then walked through the bathroom to the girls' bedroom and locked that door. Returning, she placed her handbag on the bureau and walked into Mark's arms. He had been standing staring almost absent-mindedly at the closet door, partly opened. "What is it?" Valerie asked, putting her arms around him. "What's on your mind?"

"You," he said immediately, hugging her. "Your ass. Your cunt. That's what's on my mind."

Valerie's skin pebbled lightly as the rude words stirred her juices. She snuggled her head against her husband's shoulder while his hands crept down her back and played fondly with her ungirdled behind, palpating her wide-beamed soft buttock flesh until her breath came more quickly. "I love it when you talk to me like that," she whispered.

"What's that, madam?" Mark inquired loudly. "What have you to say to your deaf old husband?"

"I said I'm in love with my husband's big prick," Valerie said clearly, and kissed him. "His lovely big prick that fucks my cunt." She looked down at the goosebumps on her arms. "Isn't it amazing what you do to me, Mark?" she asked quietly. "I'm getting wet."

"And where might that be, wife?" Mark trailed his mustache across the bare flesh of Valerie's upper arm, and she shivered.

"You know where," she retorted. "Right where your ravening monster is going to bump my little pussy."

"Let me undress you," he said huskily, and reached for the buttons on her blouse.

Valerie stood obediently while Mark slipped her out of the blouse and unfastened her bra. Her snowy white breasts crested with cherry-red nipples centered in dark areolas thrust forth firmly from her chest wall, and Mark Walker lowered his head to kiss the resilient flesh and then lick at the stiffening nipples with a probing tongue.

"Oooooooooooh!" Valerie breathed in a contented sigh. "Do you think it feels so good because I know what comes afterward will feel even better?"

"Indubitably," Mark said. He unzipped her skirt and guided it down over her hips and legs. Valerie stepped out of it and tossed it on a chair. Mark did the same with her half-slip, and Valerie stood revealed in garter belt, panties, and stockings. Teasingly Mark plucked the elasticized waistband of the panties from Valerie's slender waist and very, very slowly pulled them down over the yieldingly voluptuous milk-white globes of her outspread nude hind

11

cheeks, completely unveiled except for the ineffectively concealing garter belt tapes.

"Now let me do you," Valerie said. Mark had already removed the jacket of his suit, and she unbuttoned his shirt and pulled the tails from his trousers. She unbelted those and let them drop to his ankles, then knelt down in front of him and removed his shoes. Mark was standing with his back to the bed and Valerie's bare behind, outthrust in her kneeling position, was pointed at the closet door.

She swept his trousers from his ankles, and still kneeling, pulled down his undershorts. "Ahhhhhhh, you beautiful thing!" she said softly, taking her husband's lazy erection on her palm while with her other hand she caressed his hairy balls. Long black hair clustered thickly on Mark's thighs and buttocks. His equally hairy belly was flat and solid-looking.

Valerie wet her lips with the tip of her tongue, then lowered her head and took the prick on her palm into her mouth. She licked it, then sucked on it, her cheeks puckering. She ovaled her mouth and began to move her lips back and forth on its increasing length while the springy, full-fleshed spheres of her robustly brimful naked posterior quivered slightly from her exertions.

Mark changed the position of his feet so that he was standing sideways to the bed, and Valerie moved on her knees to remain in front of him and not lose her mouth-grip on the expanding, thick-stemmed cock crowding the back of her throat. Valerie made a humming sound deep in her throat, and the vibration passed from her lips to the prick in her mouth brought Mark up on his toes. "Christ!" he said fervently. "You've got a mouth on you like a vacuum cleaner, Val!"

Valerie let her fleshy prisoner slide from between her lips as she looked up at her husband. They were standing and kneeling, respectively, in profile to the closet. "I wish you had four more so I could bring them up for you, too," she said. "He's ready, isn't he?" She stroked the purple-headed, saliva-slick rampant prick thrusting at her face. "I adore what you're going to do to me, you darling thing."

Mark reached down and placed both hands under her armpits, raising her to her feet. Their bodies fitted together comfortably as he kissed her hard on the mouth, Valerie's softly protruding round belly blending into her husband's harder, hairy one. Just below his erection jutted upward and prodded her in the downy blond fleece atop her thigh-juncture.

They kissed lingeringly, exchanging tongues and searching out each other's mouths with darting forays. Mark's right hand groped at Valerie's thighs which widened obligingly so his hand could enter between them and a finger dip between the pink-lipped furrow nestled in her feathery curls. Valerie began to moan softly and rub her belly feverishly against Mark's.

"Ohhhh, God, I'm so hot!" she said hoarsely when Mark removed his mouth from hers. She widened her thighs still more. "Feel me, dear. Put your finger way inside."

"Let's get on the bed so I can really get at you," Mark replied. "You're almost as slippery down there as if I'd already had my prick in you."

"I just gush when you touch me," Valerie murmured. "Even with my clothes on. A couple of times I've had to change panties just before we went out somewhere."

Mark sat down on the bed and placed Valerie between his knees. He pulled the waistband of her garter belt down to mid-thigh, then let its weight pull it and her stockings down her creamy legs. He inclined her forward over one thigh almost in spanking position, then bent forward and kissed each succulent bare hind cheek. "I'm going to eat a planked steak right off your bare ass one of these

13

days," he said with a rasp in his voice. He manipulated the sleek surfaces which vibrated gently, opening and closing her deep fissure.

Once again his hand went between her thighs and a curved finger probed upward into her sex-slit. Valerie purred like a milk-fed kitten as the finger slowly worked its way in and out of her moist pussy-lips. With her left hand she reached behind her and took hold of Mark's cock which had been almost covered by her body. She squeezed it in time to the finger-frigging of her eagerly participating cunt, then gasped aloud as Mark's finger action picked up speed and intensity.

"On your back, Val!" he said sharply.

Gladly she shifted from his knees to the bed and rolled over on her back. Her splayed thighs pointed at the closet door as Mark's hand returned for a final brisk tuning-up of her sex-engine that had Valerie burbling like a teakettle.

"Ask me, sweetheart," he said finally in what had become a ritual with them.

"Please fuck me, dear," she responded. "Fuck me hard and I'll love you forever."

Mark moved in between her parted legs and, taking each in a hand, doubled them back against her chest. Valerie's finger-frictioned love nest pouted up at him from the midst of damp, blond pussy hair, and he lowered his head and ran his tongue along her reddened slit. "Ahhhhhhhhhh!" she exclaimed, stretching her thighs still farther apart. "It's just gorgeous when you eat me!"

"But it's not what you really want right now?" he questioned her.

"I want your prick in me," she said feverishly. "In my cunt. All the way in as far as it will go." Mark shuffled closer to her on his knees, and Valerie groped for his hard-

14

standing cock. "Let me put it in," she begged. "I love to put it in me."

She bumped the purple head against her cranny in search of her cuntal entrance. Her hand steadied, thrust firmly, the head disappeared, and Valerie's breath whistled between her teeth. "Ohhhhhhhh, that wonderful *feeling!*" she sighed deeply.

Mark immersed his thick cock in his wife's up-thrust quim with steady pressure. His blue-veined rigidity was engulfed in her straining twat a shining white inch at a time. He joggled his hips from side to side to widen the passage, and Valerie's lips parted again as she voiced her reaction to the sensual stimulation caused by the big prick in her sex-crevice. "Ohhhhhhhhh, Mark!" she cried. "I love you, Mark! I love you!"

When he was belly-to-belly with Valerie, Mark lowered his head to the juncture of her neck and shoulder, then began to pump upon her. His cock powerdived upon her tight-clasping cunt while all of Valerie's soft woman-flesh was in motion. Belly, breasts, and buttocks jiggled gelatinously as Mark plunged in steady strokes into his willing receptacle.

"MMMMMMMMMMMMMmmmmmmmmm!" Valerie moaned excitedly as her cunt was buffeted enjoyably by her husband's deep-lodged ramrod. "Oooooooooooh, the way—it slides—in and out is—heavenly!" She raised her legs higher and clasped Mark's waist firmly with her plump thighs, her upraised bare bottom wriggling passionately as Mark continued to plow her garden.

A hot spark ignited in her interior and proceeded to liquefy. "Mark!" Valerie half-screamed as the spark turned to a coal and the coal to a blaze. Her thighs trembled as she writhed beneath her husband's steady poking. "Mark! I'm—ohhhh!—it's good! It's—ohhh!—I'm—'m—coming, Mark! OHHHhhh!"

Her convulsed cunt deluged Mark's fleshy wedge in her body. Valerie's behind sank languidly upon the bed as her husband's cock plummeted into her juicy cavern with increasing abandon. Her hands crept down his muscled back and played lightly with his plunging buttocks, reveling in the feel of his hairiness. Mark's hard stomach resounded noisily upon Valerie's soft one as his cock penetrated her oozing chasm. Her hands left Mark's hind cheeks and her arms enfolded his upper body tightly as she felt from the increased force of his fucking of her that he was nearing his orgasm.

And then a shudder rippled through her. "Ohhhhhh?" she murmured in a questioning tone. The shudder was followed by another quick flame, fomenting sexual excitement in her hard-jostled depths. "Oooooh! Ohhhh, Mark!" Valerie panted. "I'm—wait! Ohhh, please—oooooh!—wait!"

His fierce lunges steadied to gliding thrusts as he went into a holding pattern. His wife's pearly, wide-spanned rump climbed from the bed again and jiggled in fleshy abandon. Her hips spiraled in feverishly frantic movement while her voice soared. "Mark! Mark, I'm—ooooh, there it is—again! Ahhhhh! AHHHHHHH! h-h! I'm—coming, Mark! I'm—coming again!"

Her body was wrenched by uncontrollable interior forces while his prick strokes into her returned to their former intensity. His shoulders hunched and his knees dug into the bed for additional leverage. His teeth nipped at Valerie's neck as he pounded her creaming twat, and then he bellowed hoarsely as his hands slipped beneath her to compress her bell-shaped, heavy hind cheeks while hot jets of sperm traveled the length of his prick and inundated her cock-filled jewel box.

After a moment Mark's abated erection slipped gently from his wife's ruby-red pussy-lips, and he moved out from between her legs and rolled onto his back. Valerie flexed her legs several times, savoring the diminishing sensation still lodged in her cooling cunt. Then she scrambled onto her knees and bent down over Mark, kissing his belly and running her mouth down near his greasy-looking, eroded white prick. "Thank you for waiting for me the second time, Mark," she said softly. "You're a wonderful fucker. Just wonderful."

"You're not so bad yourself—for an old lady," he teased between rapidly drawn breaths. His hands came up and recaptured her hind cheeks which showed his handprints from the frenzy of their lovemaking. "What an ass you've got on you, Val! I can never get enough of it."

"I hope you never do," Valerie returned. She licked at his shriveling cock, then sucked it. "There," she announced. "It's all clean." She licked her lips with a smacking sound. "Love that taste. Love that man-smell, too. I can get hot just thinking about the way you smell after we've made love."

"You're something else," he laughed. "I still think you're putting me on when you say you weren't getting any while you were a widow."

Valerie shook her blond head. "It's true. There were the girls, of course. And I was busy. It was too complicated. Oh, I had a proposition or two, but I never wanted just a quick poke. I wanted a husband. And now I've got one." She snuggled down against Mark with her large breasts probing his rib cage. "And you're so good to me, dear."

"What did you do all the time you were a widow, Val?"

"For relief, you mean? You know what I did. Feeling guilty as sin every time."

"Exactly what?" he persisted.

"You're making me reveal all my dreadful secrets," she protested. She wriggled closer to his warm body. "But I

17

don't really mind. I have compensation, don't I?" She placed several butterfly kisses on her husband's chest and neck. "Well, when I was absolutely climbing the wall, I'd go upstairs and remove my panties and get on the bed and play with myself with my finger while I wondered if I'd ever have a man's heavenly gristle in me again. Terribly mundane, I suppose. But also terribly mortifying to think I couldn't control my female nature."

"I'm in love with your female nature," Mark said soberly, still playing with a roomy bare buttock, slightly damp from Valerie's abandoned fucking. "So many women never realize their potentialities, Val. You do, and that's what makes it so great in the hay with you. Even the very first time—"

"Don't embarrass me by recalling that very first time, since we hadn't been churched, sir," Valerie interrupted. She raised herself and placed her blond head on Mark's chest. "But I wanted you so badly you could have had me under the main intersection traffic light if you'd pushed a little. As it was—"

"As it was your little pussy's introduction to my prick wasn't quite that public, but it didn't miss by much," Mark interrupted in his turn.

Valerie giggled. "If the choir had ever dreamed what was happening to its chaste, unsullied, prudish, angelic director, the world would have come to an end."

His big hand traced the long slope of her back and flirted with the deep crease between her billowingly fleshy hind cheeks. "How do you feel, Val?"

"Like I always feel after you fuck me so nicely," she returned promptly. "Scrumptious. Ah-ha!" Her hand darted down and encircled his re-aroused cock. "Look who's sitting up and taking notice!" She half-turned to place her head above his middle and lipped the lengthening fleshy rod into her mouth. Then she dropped it. "Perhaps you'd rather not?" she asked. "I don't mean to be an absolute pig, dear."

"Go right ahead," he invited her. "But this time I want to backdoor you."

"Any way you want," she answered. "Any way at all. Kneeling on the bed or standing up and bending over?"

"Standing up. There's an extraordinary tactile sensation when I get my prick between those handsome big ass-cheeks of yours, Val."

"My most fervent wish is that you never run out of sensations, Mark," Valerie said earnestly. "And you never will if I can help it." She dropped her mouth upon the stiffening prick and swirled her tongue around its reddish-purple head. It delighted her when she felt Mark's thigh muscles tense from the titillation afforded by her quick-darting tongue.

She rose to her knees to get more leverage, her croup pointed at Mark's face. He played idly with her velvety globes while Valerie mouth-fucked his long cock into its former state of massive engorgement. He parted her weighty nude haunches with his knuckles and slipped a finger into her lubricious cunt-hole which he proceeded to palpitate thrillingly while little tremors ran through Valerie's luscious belly and thighs.

"You're on the verge of overdoing it, sweetheart," he said finally, and Valerie reluctantly removed her hard-working mouth from his saliva-slippery big prick. The circumcised, purple-eyed head pointed right at her chin. She gave it a parting lick and slid from the bed.

She pulled the night table slightly away from the bed, removed the telephone and placed it on the floor, then plumped a pillow up and covered the small table's top with it. She widened her leg stance to correspond with the table's legs and lowered herself upon the pillow on her stomach so that her tautly curved bottom cheeks thrust backward invit-ingly. "Come and get it, dear," she said over her shoulder.

Mark climbed from the bed and approached her plumped-out, deliriously capacious nudity. He stood behind her for a moment rubbing his belly against the satiny skin of her backside, then brought his erection up between her part-ed thighs. Valerie sighed with pleasure as her husband skill-fully found her slot and inserted the head of his straining prick inside, then bucked its thick-stemmed length all the way up her sex-channel.

"Mmmmmmmmmm!" Valerie moaned as she felt Mark's balls collide with her upper thighs as the head of his prick seemed to reach well up into her molten-lava interior. "That's—so nice!"

She adored the feeling of distention, although the position wasn't her favorite for fucking. She found it diffi-cult to come, but anything Mark wanted to do in bed was perfectly all right with her. He certainly made her come often enough in other positions. She relaxed her stomach and buttock muscles and half-closed her eyes as the thick prick began to surge up into her from beneath. Mark's lunges into her cunt were so powerful that two-thirds of the time Valerie came up on her toes. The steady thwacking noise of his belly against her bare behind was the only sound in the motel room.

Valerie floated tranquilly in a cozy sexual haze. She already knew she wasn't going to come, but she didn't care. The big prick pistoned her sex-chute with felicitous aban-don as Mark's heavy breathing testified to his expenditure of effort. His hands which had been gripping her bare shoul-ders slipped down and locked underneath the round bowl of her—lissome stomach, pulling her up against him more tightly.

"Hold—on!" Mark's voice rasped as his metronom-ic fucking of his wife disintegrated into a rabbitlike convulsion of his hips as he spurted his thick cream far up into her crammed incision. "Ahhhhhhh, Jesus!" he sighed deeply, resting his entire weight along the length of her back. "What a fuck!"

Valerie could feel the formerly ravaging cock drooping within her, unplugging her cunt-hole so that she could feel Mark's spend escaping from her pussy and trickling down her thighs. Her husband's weight was considerable but, supported as she was by the table, not onerous. She rested quietly and listened to his breathing slack off to normal.

Finally he pulled his withered prong out of her, slapped a rotund naked hind cheek in affectionate thanks for service rendered, and sank back upon the nearby bed. Valerie raised herself from the pillow-cushioned table top, took a quick swipe between her legs with the trailing edge of a sheet, then joined her husband on the bed. They stretched lengthily with mutually repleted sighs, Mark's back to Valerie's front with her back to the closet door.

Valerie kissed the nape of Mark's neck and the tip of his uppermost shoulder. He reached behind him and once more captured a handful of spherical sleekness which always seemed to enthrall him. "Mark," Valerie broke the comfortable silence. "I hate to say it, but the girls will be coming back from their shopping trip."

"Where do you suppose I could send them this time?" he asked lazily.

Valerie laughed happily, a cheery, high-spirited, gleeful sound. "Listen, Superman," she chided him playfully, "we're supposed to check out of this motel and head for home."

"I suppose so," he sighed. "D'you want to use the shower first?"

"We could use it together," Valerie said archly.

He chuckled deeply. "I think our check-out time would be further delayed if we did, sweetheart."

She raised herself on one elbow to trail her lips lovingly across her husband's bare shoulder. A moving shadow on the wall caught her eye, and at the same time she sensed rather than saw a flicker of movement behind her. Valerie turned her head, and froze.

Tiptoeing from the opened closet door in their stockinged feet, carrying their shoes, were her daughters, Ethel and Penny. The girls flitted silently through the motel room into the adjoining bathroom which connected with their own bedroom. Valerie heard the faint click of a latched door.

In that first quick glimpse Valerie thought her heart had stopped beating. She was afraid she was going to faint. Then adrenalin-charged blood thudded through her veins in violent emotional reaction. "Mark!" she got out in a choked voice from a throat that felt both dry and constricted. "Oh, Mark!"

He flopped over instantly, turning to face her. "What is it, Val? Leg cramp? Let me rub it."

"Ohhhh, n-no!" she whimpered. Her lungs felt seared; she had no breath. "The girls—" She couldn't bring herself to say it.

He looked at his watch. "You're right. We probably should get going."

She buried her face in his hairy chest, unable to look him in the face. "The girls were in the c-closet, Mark, watching! They s-saw what I d-did!" She drew a long, quivering breath. "They heard what I s-said! Ohhhh, Mark, what am I going to do?"

"Whale their asses," he said promptly. "But are you sure? I didn't see or hear a thing."

22

"I *saw* them," Valerie moaned miserably. "Oh, God, I frenched you, and—and the things we said—" She started to cry, great choking sobs that racked her plump body.

Mark took her in his arms comfortingly.

"Goddammit, I'm not going to have them spoiling our relationship!" he said irritably.

Valerie tried to catch her sobbing breath. "H-how am I going to make them understand that the s-self-restraint I've been—I've been preaching to them d-doesn't apply to a m-married woman in bed with her h-husband!" she wailed.

"Smart-assed little dumplings, aren't they?" Mark said. "Listen, we can't let them get away with it. I'm not going to have you skulking around ashamed to look them in the face. We'll go in their room right now and pin the tail on those donkeys. I'll do the talking. And the acting, if necessary. We'll play it by ear. You just back me up."

He placed an arm firmly around his wife's shaking shoulders, assisted her to her feet, and began handing her the scattered articles of clothing from his undressing of her.

CHAPTER II

Mark Walker barely repressed a smile as he hurried into his own clothes and then handed Valerie her dress. "We can't let them get away with it, Val," he repeated. "Otherwise they'll have you feeling you did wrong instead of them."

He watched impatiently as his wife, red-eyed and still sniffling, pulled the dress over her head. He really enjoyed her full-bodied sensuality, but he was eager to begin reaping the secondary fruits of his marriage to her. He had deliberately planted the thought of watching in her daughters' minds that morning, although hardly daring to hope that it would bear fruit so quickly. Still, he had obviously underestimated Ethel, she of the mercurial moods ranging from sullen to vivacious. It was Ethel who had been the ringleader, he was sure; Penny was just an easily-led little round-bottomed dumpling.

He had noticed the partly opened closet door as soon as they re-entered their motel bedroom, and while not entirely sure of the girls' presence he had made sure to make the lovemaking an eye-opener in case they actually were watching. He had posed Valerie several times with an eye to her greater exposure as witnessed from the closet, and he had encouraged her to greater verbal and bodily abandon, an exercise to which her own ardent nature had libidinously contributed.

"Do you think they know you saw them?" he asked as Valerie smoothed down her dress.

"I h-have no idea," she responded shakily. She scrubbed at her eyes with her knuckles. "Give me a m-minute to wash my face, Mark," she pleaded. "I c-can't confront them l-looking like this." She went into the bathroom, ran the cold water, and laved her face and eyes with the washcloth.

"Ready?" he asked with as much restraint as he could manage.

"Y-yes," she said almost in a whisper after a final glance at her tear-wet eyes in the mirror. She couldn't seem to turn off the tears after the shock of the realization that her daughters had seen her and Mark in such hedonistic carnality no matter how lovingly and mutually congenial.

Mark brushed past her in the bathroom and opened the door of the girls' bedroom without knocking. He strode inside, stern-faced, and Valerie followed a shrinking two paces behind. The girls were seated in armchairs on opposite sides of the room and, knowing her daughters from babyhood, Valerie would have known their guilt even if she hadn't actually seen them emerging from the closet. Penny looked the image of panic-stricken guilt; Ethel that of glacial defiance.

Just months short of her seventeenth birthday, Ethel Walker was an inch taller than her mother with a svelte frame repeating Valerie's lush curves in delightful miniature. Shoulder-length auburn hair caught and reflected the light which also pointed out the light dusting of facial freckles which Valerie knew was continued on her daughter's body. The strong-minded Ethel had often taxed Valerie's patience with attempted rebellions against Valerie's restraints. Ethel considered her mother hopelessly old-fashioned, and Valerie knew that the girl had been amazed when her mother captivated the sophisticated Mark. She should certainly have revised her old-fashioned name tag after what she saw, Valerie thought grimly, her anger at the invasion of her privacy sweeping away part of her mortification as she looked at her older daughter attractively clad in a print dress. Ethel had good clothes sense.

Valerie shifted her attention to the other armchair. Penny, a year and three days younger than Ethel, sat huddled in her armchair with one hand pressed apprehensively to her lips. Clad in faded jeans that hugged her chubby curves, the younger girl was a sweet-faced, sweet-natured youngster but so easily led that she reminded Valerie of herself in her own youth. Shining, jet-black hair framed the youthful features, emphasizing the beautiful skin and slightly turned-up nose. Soft brown eyes were fixed anxiously upon her stepfather, whom the girl had confessed to Valerie was the handsomest man Penny had ever seen.

Mark had paused in the center of the room, theatrically heightening the tension of the moment. When he spoke finally, his voice was so vibrantly harsh that Valerie felt a little chill along her own spine. "Am I to believe that you two girls just injudiciously invaded the sanctity of the marriage bedroom?" he blared at them. "Is it true?" He was staring at the younger girl.

Penny winced visibly. She couldn't find her voice, but nodded helplessly. Tears puddled in her brown eyes, then ran down her cheeks. Her small hands knitted themselves together tightly in her lap.

"What did you think you were doing?" Mark roared.

The girl swallowed hard. "You said—you said mother was h-happy," she whispered, "and I thought—Ethel s-said if we watched we could s-see."

In the other armchair Ethel's chin rose disdainfully at this betrayal of her leadership. Her eyes were fixed on space midway between Mark and Valerie.

Mark's voice quieted suddenly. "But you knew you were doing wrong," he said to Penny.

The girl burst into wrenching sobs, sprang to her feet, and started to run to her mother. Mark extended a pointed finger at her, and Penny stopped as though she had run into a wall. "We—I didn't th-think it would be l-like that," she sobbed. "I th-thought you'd be k-kissing and—and—" Fresh tears swallowed up her words.

Looking at Valerie's face, Mark knew he had done well to prevent Penny from fleeing to her mother's arms. Compassion was writ large upon Valerie's expressive features, and immediate compassion would have interfered with his plans. He sat down in the armchair Penny had just vacated and patted his thigh. "Come here and get over my knee," he ordered sternly. "Girls who act like children will be treated like children."

"Oooooooh!" Penny wailed in dismay when his meaning became clear to her. Her glance streaked to Valerie. "Must I, mother?"

Valerie hesitated. She would have had no qualms if it had been Ethel about to go over Mark's knees. She groped for a method to differentiate between her daughters' behavior but could come up with nothing. "Yes, you must," she said reluctantly.

Weeping, Penny obediently turned to Mark, who promptly extended her face down across his knees with her chubby buttocks in their oft-washed jeans pointing at the others in the motel room. "Unfasten your belt," he commanded.

He was already unzipping the jeans' side fastening while Penny raised her round stomach and released her belt buckle. Mark at once began to pull the jeans down over the girl's bulging backside, deliberately making slow going of it. His hand alternately fumbled with back and front of the jeans as he tugged downward first in front and then in back. With the jeans part way down and the upper slopes of her white-pantied bottom exposed, Penny gasped as Mark's knuckles grazed her bare stomach.

The jeans slid away suddenly and descended down Penny's tubby thighs, disclosing all of her tight-pantied rear. The girl whimpered as Mark's big hand immediately descended upon the waistband of the panties and the slow unveiling continued. Valerie watched sympathetically as

Penny's sobs were renewed while the white panties crept downward over her bottom, revealing the flawless white skin and dimpled amplitudes of her chubby bare behind. From her armchair, Ethel glanced quickly at her sister's exposure, then looked away as the tip of her tongue circled her lips.

Valerie was amazed at the expanse of Penny's posterior ... why, the girl looked like a woman with her full-fleshed globes divided by her deep crevice. It was altogether different from seeing her daughter in the shower occasionally.

Mark moved his thighs under Penny's stomach and her backside trembled as a tuft of thick black hair appeared far down between her clenched thighs.

"This is the way children are treated!" Mark announced in his deep baritone, and spanked a soft globe that rebounded with a quiver. He waited seven or eight seconds before he slapped its twin stingingly.

"Ouch!" Penny muttered, wriggling her smarting fanny.

Almost in slow motion Mark spanked each nude hind cheek again, the loud reports of his palm on the girl's tender seat resounding noisily.

"Oww!" Penny whimpered as Mark did it again. "Owww!" Her thighs widened as she tried to rotate her backside out from under the smarting palm, revealing flashing glimpses of her chubby pink-lipped pussy nestled in its furry embrasure to the watching eyes in the room. "Owwwww! Oooooooh!" Her agitated buttocks turned from pink to scarlet.

"All right!" Mark said after perhaps the twentieth spank. "Go and apologize to your mother!"

Penny wriggled from his knees thankfully, and with no thought of her exposure, trotted to Valerie while clutching her hampering down-drawn panties and jeans at mid-thigh. "Ohhhhhh, m-mother!" the girl wailed, throwing herself into Valerie's arms. "I'm so s-sorry I did it! I never *d-dreamed* of em—embarrassing y-you!"

Valerie found herself instinctively patting the spank-warmed, glowing bottom-cheeks at which Mark was staring from his armchair. Well, if I was a man I'd probably stare, too, Valerie thought. "Pull up your panties, dear," she whispered to the sobbing Penny. "It's all right."

Penny's face turned as crimson as her backside as she hastily pulled up the drooping panties. Mark sat back in his chair, satisfied. It wasn't his purpose to spank so hard the girls would be reduced to shrieking helplessly from the pain in their flaming seats. No, his plan was different. He intended to make the spankings look good in front of Valerie while in reality his efforts were directed at making the girls' exposure so great that when they had time to think it over afterward there would be no chance of their feeling body-shyness with him in the future.

He crooked a finger at Ethel, frozen in her chair. "You," he said. "Come over here."

She sat rigidly, her eyes flicking from Penny gingerly stuffing her plumpness back into her tight jeans to her mother to whom Ethel couldn't bring herself to appeal. Watching in amazement from the closet at her mother's licentiously bawdy performance in bed with her husband, Ethel had thought with satisfaction that she had rid herself for all time of the moralizing preachments from Valerie which had so exasperated the older daughter. Now the tables were turned somehow, and it was she and Penny who were being shamefully humiliated.

"If I have to come over there and get you," Mark Walker said calmly, "you'll remember for three days that you could have walked over here."

Ethel shivered at the implied threat. Her own bottom had quaked in sympathy with each pistol-like report of

Mark's big hand upon her sister's bare flesh. Now she was being coerced into assisting at her own abashed disgrace. But the threat was too real, too imminent, to ignore. She rose to her feet on legs that trembled and approached her stepfather's chair.

Mark wasted no time. He turned Ethel around as he had Penny and doubled the tall-bodied girl up over his knees. He raised her skirt deliberately, folded it twice and deposited it in the middle of her back, then did the same with her slip. Ethel wriggled uneasily, and Valerie stared in surprise at pale blue bikini panties which were Ethel's only remaining covering. Where on earth had they come from, she wondered? Then she recalled the morning's shopping expedition. Trust Ethel to go to extremes.

The crotch-band of the thin material was so narrow that Valerie could see curling tendrils of reddish-brown hair escaping on either side at the base of Ethel's slender thighs. Mark reached for the waistband of the bikini panties, and Ethel's resolve broke. "Please!" she begged. "Not bare!" And then with more of her usual defiance: "You don't have to make a holy show out of me!"

"What makes you think you should be treated any differently than your sister?" Mark inquired, and he leisurely pulled her panties down. Ethel's behind, lacking Penny's dimples and bouncing amplitude, was still sweetly made. Mark gazed down with inward glee at the smooth, velvety surface of gracefully elegant hind cheeks swelling flower-like from a slender waist. Ethel was a miniaturized version of her mother's womanliness, as Mark instantly recognized.

He began to spank the older girl, and the loud smacks of his palm distressed Ethel almost as much as the quick blaze her stepfather ignited in her soft body-cushions. It sounded so childish! But the increasing conflagration setting her writhing naked bottom aflame soon made her forget her embarrassment about the sound. "Ohh!" she gasped at each burning spank. "Ohhh! Ohhh!" She wriggled furiously all over Mark's knees, disclosing her peach-colored slit and reddish-brown mossy grotto.

Mark suddenly gripped Ethel's left buttock and separated it from its twin, disclosing the paler puckering of her anus as he delivered three final spanks to the girl's quiveringly blushing right buttock. "Now go and apologize to your mother!" he ordered, releasing her. "And decently, or you'll be right back down here again."

Ethel rose from his knees stiffly, trying to restrain her tears. Ignoring the pale blue bikini panties which had descended to her calves during her struggles to escape the scorching palm, the girl hurriedly pulled down her slip and dress to conceal her semi-nudity, but not before she knew her stepfather had an eyeful of her bare belly and the feathery red curls dipping into her thigh-juncture.

Lips compressed tremulously, Ethel shuffled to her mother, hobbled by the down-dropped panties but unwilling to stoop before everyone and pull them up. "I'm sorry, mother," she managed to say in a strangled voice. "I—I shouldn't have done it."

"Satisfactory?" Mark asked Valerie. She nodded, and Mark clapped his hands together so sharply that both girls jumped. "All right," he said briskly. "We're checking out in half an hour, and I want everyone ready. And let's act like human beings on the ride home or we could do this all over again." He fixed each girl in turn with a stern stare before turning to his wife. "Coming, Val?" Without waiting for her reply he walked through the bathroom between the bedrooms.

Valerie followed him and closed their bedroom door. At the sound of the click of the latch, Mark turned to her in pretended anxiety. "Did I overdo it?" he asked. "Did I lay it on them too hard?"

"If anything, you underdid it," Valerie informed him. "Considering the offense. I'd have used a hairbrush and you'd have really heard them squeak."

"I'm not used to the female behind in that position," Mark said. "I was afraid of really hurting them."

"A girl's seat is tougher than you realize," Valerie replied. She tried to smile and found her face stiff. "I'll bet neither of them is more than light pink right now. But you really had the right idea, Mark. When we went in there, I thought I'd never be able to hold my head up in front of them again. Now somehow I have my dignity back. Although it's never going to be the same, of course."

"Some day you'll be able to look back on this and laugh about it," Mark predicted.

"Never!" Valerie returned indignantly. "When I think of what I did, and said, and what you did—" Color flooded up into her features, heightening their attractiveness.

Mark put his arm around her and kissed her on the lips warmly. It was a brotherly, affectionate kiss, not a passionate one, and Valerie responded in kind as her entire body seemed to relax for the first time since she had seen the girls over her shoulder. "Oh, Mark, I love you so much!" she murmured in a voice that quavered despite herself.

He winked at her. "Care to prove it, madam?"

She smiled at him as a warm tide of feeling for this attractive man seemed to banish the body chill she had felt previously. "Not right now, sir," she replied in familiar reversion to her role of demure housewife. "But please ask me again when I've had time to pull myself together."

Mark kissed her again, and Valerie sighed contentedly.

Somehow the nightmare had evaporated.

In the other bedroom Penny Walker watched her sister Ethel pulling the bikini panties up her long legs and over her dusty-pink sleek-looking hindquarters. "Boy, we really got off easy!" the younger girl said fervently. "I thought we were going to get blistered." She rubbed her bottom gently with both palms over her jeans. "How's your behind, Ethel?"

"Perfectly all right," the older girl said crisply as though by the inaccuracy she could deny to herself that her humiliation had ever taken place. "You realize of course that your mother's husband—" She managed to make it sound like a curse word. "—was having a field day seeing what he could see."

"I don't care one single bit what he could see," Penny said candidly. "He could have burned us up, and he didn't."

"And what do you think of your saintly mother now with her mealy-mouthed preaching about ladylike behavior and—"

Penny clapped her hands over her ears. "I'm not going to listen to you, Ethel," she warned. "Mother was happy, and Mark was h-happy—" She started to sniffle. "And w-we were perfect *beasts* to do what we did!"

"Oh, blow your nose!" Ethel exclaimed in irritation.

Penny uncovered her ears. "Listen, I don't know about you, but when they knock on the door I'm going to be ready."

She found her overnight bag and began packing it.

Valerie and Mark were seated on the chaise longue in front of a gas-log fireplace in the den of Mark's spacious home at eleven o'clock that night. Mark had a Scotch-and-water in his hand and Valerie had a green creme de menthe on the rocks on the floor beside her slippered feet. Mark glanced at his wife appraisingly as he removed his glass from his lips after taking a swallow. "Well, how do you feel now that the shit has stopped hitting the fan, Val, as we say around the office?" he asked lazily.

She slid down the chaise longue until she could rest her head on his shoulder. "Much better, husband," she said softly.

"I'd say your nerves are in better shape," he agreed. "You can't let those kids get you down, you know. Even if they did see—"

She placed a finger over his lips. "I still don't like to even think about what they saw," she interrupted him.

"But we've got a right, Val," he argued. "A perfect right. Whose business is it but ours?" He took another swallow from his glass. "The fact they chose to take a peek doesn't alter the essential fact that it's none of their business." He grinned suddenly. "A fact I believe they'd take an oath to after the waxing I gave their asses."

He sobered. "Speaking of asses, I was startled at the development of both of them at their ages."

"I guess I was nearly as surprised as you were," Valerie admitted.

Mark turned his head and kissed her on the cheek. "With three like that—" He reached down and patted Valerie's backside. "On the premises I can see where Mark Walker has a good chance of developing into an ass-freak. I'll be the one hiding in closets for a look."

Valerie smiled as she returned his kiss. "You won't have to hide to get a look at one of them," she promised.

He patted her again, then raised an eyebrow. "Hmmmm? No girdle, wifie?"

"I never wear one in the house," Valerie confessed. "I guess I'm always hoping you'll feel like playing with something a girdle would only interfere with."

He laughed so hard he almost spilled the rest of his drink. "Now I wonder exactly what that could be?" he inquired with mock solemnity when his chuckles ceased.

"Anything covered by a girdle, sir."

"Like this?" His hand dipped under her skirt, raced up between her thighs, and massaged the thin-materialed panties snugged to her crotch.

Valerie shivered deliciously. "Well, a pantie-girdle anyway," she said. The expression on her wholesomely pretty face changed as the finger continued to massage her. "Let me take them off, Mark," she whispered. "I'll only get them wet."

She raised herself on her knees, skinned the panties downward after .holding her skirt up out of the way, then sat down on the chaise longue again to pull them completely off over her ankles. Mark immediately pulled her across his lap, bottom side up, folded her skirt and slip out of the way, and filled both hands with the springy-solid nude amplitudes of her sleek-looking hind cheeks. Valerie rested on the chaise with her head to Mark's left and her feet to his right with a dreamy little smile on her lips as he fondled, cuddled, and lightly smacked her milk-white globes.

She stirred only when he parted her gratifyingly luxurious croup-cheeks and fingered the depths of her plunging crevice. "You little sinner, you're wet already," he told her then.

Valerie fluttered the muscles in her thighs in pleasurable enjoyment. "I'm always wet when I'm near you, Mark," she murmured with her head pressed into the chaise while the probing finger parted her blond curls and slipped inside her moist pussy-lips. "Sometimes when you just look at me across a room I get wet."

He lifted her upright and sat her on his lap, and Valerie put her arms around his neck. "What in the world were you like at seventeen?" he asked curiously.

"I was married at seventeen," she said soberly. "Three months pregnant. To the boy next door, because I was always easily stirred. It's one reason I've probably been a little too strict with the girls."

"In reaction," he agreed. "How did it happen?"

"Oh, the usual way, I guess." Valerie thought for a moment as she looked back down the years. "We'd always paired off when we were kids. I guess we must have been about eleven when we went through the I'll-show-you-mine-if-you'll-show-me-yours syndrome in his cellar one rainy afternoon. Then he became interested in athletics and I didn't see as much of him. Until one rainy afternoon in my cellar—"

She paused. "Why do so many sexual things happen on rainy afternoons, do you suppose?" she asked.

"Because if it was clear kids would be outside playing," Mark replied. "You were saying?"

"Yes. I was washing out a pair of my father's overalls in the basement washtubs when Jack came down the outside cellarway. He was smoking a cigarette, and I took a couple of puffs. Then he started to—you know—snuggle. I let him go, thinking I had everything under control. Then it was as though an electric current ran through me all at once, and our hands bumped together as we both tried to take down my panties. He screwed me on an old door set up on two sawhorses. Hardly a comfortable initiation, but at that age it's good on a picket fence."

"It will probably be the major regret of my life that I didn't get your cherry," Mark said into her ear.

"I think they're an overrated commodity," Valerie said. "Messy, and the girl cries afterward."

"I wonder if they do today?" Mark said. "I'd think the majority were a little more tough-minded in this day and age." He eased a hand under Valerie's dress, bunched on her thighs, and began to rub the smooth bowl of her naked stomach. "So what happened?"

"The classic pattern," Valerie replied. "We did it three or four more times that month, and then I missed my period. From the date Ethel was born, I was probably caught that very first time. My folks nearly went wild. My father paddled me purple when my mother told him after I told her. I never forgave him for that. What was I going to change then?" She was silent for a moment, eyes fixed broodingly across the room as the big warm hand continued to stroke her belly. "So we had to get married."

"And it wasn't successful?"

Valerie hesitated, again looking backward. "Oh, it was probably moderately successful. When we were in bed, anyway. Which is a stupid thing to say, but the truth. We never had much except that in common. My mother didn't speak to me for a month when I told her I was carrying Penny so soon after Ethel was born. I guess she thought she had a doe rabbit for a daughter. Now they're both gone, and Jack's gone. He was hurt at the factory, and one of the things affected was his privates. It didn't seem serious at first, but it was never much fun for him after that. Then his condition worsened and I nursed him for two years before he died." She was silent again before resuming with a sigh. "It all seems so long ago."

"But it wasn't," Mark pointed out. "You're only twice Ethel's age now. But I never realized you'd been without sex for almost ten years when I met you."

"Until you caught me in the choir loft," Valerie agreed.

"That famous day," Mark chuckled. "In the space behind the organ with the choir practicing on the other side of the partition. Would you believe I attended choir practice that day not only with malice aforethought but with a plan?"

"Really? I thought it was an accident. Like being struck by lightning." Valerie smiled. "It felt like being struck by lightning."

"I couldn't get at you at your home," Mark explained. "The girls were almost always around. I couldn't coax you out of town for a motel weekend. You primly rejected the idea. It was driving me crazy that I couldn't get next to the genteel, refined, sedate, demure big-assed female whom I was positive was a hot piece of goods."

"I was always so afraid of letting that part of my nature show. It seemed—you know—disgraceful. Animalistic."

"But then when I finally cornered you—"

"Ooooooh, my!" Valerie sighed. "I'll never forget it. You were ruthless, and I loved it. Brutal, and I loved it even more. I get squirmy just thinking about it now."

She slid from his la-p, unzipped his trousers, and removed from his shorts his straining white prick she had felt nudging the backs of her thighs. She bent down over his lap and took the reddish-purple head in her mouth, tickling it with her tongue and sucking at it with in-drawn cheeks, then rubbing her ovalled lips along as much of the length as she could get inside her mouth. Mark's hand once again slipped beneath her skirt and slip and played with her nude rump.

"How about a fuck in front of the fire?" he asked finally. "Or are you afraid one of the girls might come downstairs?"

"Let's call them," Valerie said wickedly, then giggled. "No, I'm not nearly that brave. But we're safe. They're both asleep. I looked in at them before I came downstairs just now."

"Then you're for it, Madam Wife," Mark said firmly. "Shape up the racetrack so the horse can trot."

They rose from the chaise and finished undressing. Mark arranged the chaise's pillows in a row on the floor in front of the gas-log. Valerie's firm, voluminous white curves were marbled in the flickering light as Mark put her on her back on the cushions. He parted her legs, and the light glistened on her pale fleece and the paler flesh beneath it. He moved on his knees between her legs, and when he crouched down over her, Valerie reached for his blunt-headed, thick-stemmed long cock and applied its tip to her dewy cuntal-chasm. She raised her legs higher as Mark leaned slowly down into her.

The big white blue-veined prick slid gradually into Valerie's constricting pussy-sheath while Mark, balanced on his hands above her glossy belly, stared down at her face, half-peaceful, half-excited. He joggled his hips, and Valerie's breath whistled in what was almost a squeal.

"Ohhhhhh, Mark!" she moaned, tightening her thighs and clasping her heels together over his back.

"Ask me, sweetheart," he said in the familiar ritual.

"Please fuck me, dear," she responded at once. "Fuck me hard and I'll love you forever."

He lowered his upper body onto the deliciously malleable platform of her warm belly and large, ruby-nippled breasts, then began to swoop in and out of her. In less than a minute he was burying his big prick to the hilt in every wallowing plunge upon Valerie's uptilted love-trench. Her breath hissed and burbled-between her half-parted lips as her heavy hind cheeks bored upward agitatedly while flurrying and churning as her feverishly inflamed cunt engulfed the steady-stroking long cock.

"Mark!" she gasped. "Ohh, Mark!" Her voice turned shrill as her uplifted bare backside twitched and palpitated in a series of throbbing jerks. "Ooooooooooh, I'm coming, Mark! I'm—*ohhh!—commming!* OHHH-h-h-h-h!!"

40

He tucked his head in the juncture of her neck and shoulder as her wild-plunging buttocks slowed to a peacefully placid jogging movement. Her hands roamed languidly from his tufted shoulders to his hairy backside as he slammed his hardened rigidity in and out of her streaming cunt. Perspiration dripped from his matted chest onto her breasts, and additional perspiration between their bodies caused their stomachs to part after each of his fierce lunges with a faint sucking sound.

"Love-ly, love-ly, love-ly!" Valerie murmured as the hard prick bored into her soft chalice. "Oh, Mark, if it's only—as good—for you!"

His hips went out of control as hot jets of jism shot up his prick and deluged Valerie's already dripping sex-fissure. "Agggrrrhhh!" he snarled as he creamed her with his boiling load. They rested in each other's arms, both feeling the dwindling descent of his prick in her slot. It finally fell out itself with a soft plopping noise, and they both laughed.

Mark rose and helped Valerie up from the cushions. She wiped herself and him with her panties, then picked up their discarded clothing. Mark stood her up on the chaise, then crouched in front of her and picked her up on his shoulders. Valerie rode him upstairs with her legs over his shoulders and her damp pussy rubbing the back of his neck. "Quiet!" she kept murmuring as he bumped into things. "Quiet!" Then a fit of giggling overtook her.

Mark dumped her onto their bed, rolled in beside her, and they fell asleep in each other's arms.

CHAPTER III

Valerie overslept in the morning.

Sunlight was pouring in the bedroom windows when she finally opened her eyes. She looked instinctively at the other side of the bed, but it was empty. Mark was both an early riser and an early-to-the-office man.

She looked next at the bureau mirror, their bulletin board, and saw the familiar square of white paper slipped between glass and wood in one corner. She yawned, knuckled her eyes, sat up, and reluctantly extended her feet to the floor. She walked to the bureau in the gossamer nightgown which had been one of Mark's presents to her, a gown so sheer that fleeting suggestions of Valerie's cranberry-red teats and mossy mound showed through it.

As usual, Mark's message was brief. "Home for dinner, sweetheart." Valerie's eyes lingered on the final word. It was his favorite endearment for her, and the one she cherished most. Smiling, she put on a robe and went downstairs. It was Ethel's morning for tennis, and she assumed that Penny, a congenital late sleeper, was still in her bedroom.

The first thing Valerie saw when she entered the living room was the cushions from the chaise longue still lined up in a row in front of the fireplace where she and Mark had forgotten them the previous evening. Her cheeks pinkened as she wondered if Ethel had seen them and made the correct deduction. She replaced them on the chaise, then sat down and stared introspectively at the fireplace.

In her mind's eye she re-created the scene from last night: two naked bodies on the chaise cushions, the one glisteningly white and juicily plump, the other muscularly hard and masculinely hirsute, welded together in sexual frenzy. The picture stirred her; her fingers curled until her nails bit into her palms. Was that what Ethel had seen mentally if she saw the lined-up cushions this morning?

Valerie decided suddenly that she didn't care. It had been horribly embarrassing yesterday to discover oneself under observation in the heat of the moment in the motel room, but wasn't Mark right about it? They loved each other, and who had a better right to demonstrate their love in any manner they saw fit? Not too many women could make their husbands as happy as she tried to make Mark, Valerie comforted herself.

She recalled his reference to their very first session together, and her features glowed at the remembrance. She shook her blond head in fond recollection. His wanting her hadn't come as a surprise—it rarely does to any woman, she reflected—but the occasion was surely a tribute to Mark's daring and boldly executed strategy.

Mark Walker had wangled an introduction to Valerie very shortly after his first appearance at church as a newcomer in town. The handsome grass widower had been the cynosure of all eyes, but he had had none himself except for Valerie. He pursued her steadily with invitations only half of which she accepted, and proposed to her in the third week of their acquaintanceship.

She had put him off, both flattered and flustered. The man's vibrant masculinity made her feel physically weak in his close presence. She wasn't sure she wanted this whirlwindish male animal in her ordered, manless life. After all, she had done without a man for years, despite feminine itchings. And very nicely, thank you, she told herself proudly.

And then with one bold stroke Mark had made her speculations about herself and her future moot. He had appeared at choir practice one evening, surprisingly since he admitted to having no voice. He had joked with her about it when she first asked him if he cared to join the choir. "Only if you have a part for a bullfrog," he answered.

44

But there he was, in the choir loft that night, smiling and moving toward her. Little Letitia Hogan was at the organ, and Valerie was wielding the baton. Mark beckoned to her, and she tapped the baton on the music stand, bringing the chorus to a ragged halt. "From the beginning, please," she said, handed the baton to her assistant to conduct the score, and walked toward Mark.

"You're looking more beautiful than ever this evening," he began.

"I'm sure you didn't come here this evening just to tell me that, Mark," she replied. For the first two weeks of their acquaintanceship she had called him Mr. Walker. She felt a wariness with the man. She had already successfully fended off an attempted coup upon her person in her own home. She didn't hold it against him, since he had offered no force, and this was the substructure of the male nature. But if and when she succumbed—accepted his offer of marriage, that is—it would be upon her own terms, she had long since decided.

"I came about the church organ," he said. He turned her about until she was facing it. "I'm something of an amateur organ buff, and this one is rather unique." He gestured largely toward the sweeping bank of organ pipes above Letitia Hogan's gray head. "I wonder if there's the usual room at the rear where I might examine the interior piping and the electronic bellows?"

"Why, yes, there is," she conceded, pointing out the small door.

"Will I need a guide?" he inquired.

"I'll be glad to show you, Mark," she answered, and motioned for her assistant to continue with the full score.

She entered the cramped space behind the thin partition and turned on the single unshaded light bulb. When she turned, Mark had closed the door and was but a step away from her. Before she had a chance to divine his intention, he took her in his arms. Then his hard lips were impressed firmly upon her soft mouth while one arm held her easily and the other hand roamed her body, her breasts, her buttocks, her thighs. She couldn't free her mouth from his passionately sportive lips and questing tongue, and when she felt his hand rucking up her skirt she was unable to pivot away from the probing fingers and palm which cupped the whole of her plump sex in her girdle-opening.

He had her half-undressed while she was still trying to free herself from the fiery tongue and ardent mouth which stirred her to her toes. Above their heads the organ pipes wheezed, rattled, and groaned, the bass notes setting off vibrations which trembled the floor under their feet. Valerie gasped as the searching mouth disappeared while he was ridding her of her girdle and the hard masculine hands laved her luxuriantly supple fan-shaped nude buttock cheeks. She felt as if she were suffocating in the intensity of her mingled emotions.

He unzipped his trousers and placed in her hand an erection whose size made her knees quake. She looked down at it instinctively, hating herself at once for the unladylike betrayal of her arousal. The purple-headed monster with its throbbing blue veins winked up at her, and she swallowed hard.

She felt like a rag doll as Mark turned her about and doubled her over. He crowded up behind her under the glaring light bulb and the rampant big prick prodded her flinching thigh-juncture. He had it into her squirming cunt so expertly and so quickly that half its lovely gristle was imbedded in her before she could draw a second breath.

She had never been fucked from the rear standing up, and she wouldn't have believed she could enjoy it. Her naked bottom was chafed briskly by his trouser-front as he rammed her so hard he moved her across the narrow space. Her long-virgin cunt-sheath felt unbearably distended yet hotly functional from the riotous gusto of its ravishment. She came twice with jerking accompaniments by her stomach muscles before she felt his meaty prong savagely deluge her still-twitching sex-slit. She almost fell when he pulled out of her.

He turned her around, straightened her up, and kissed her gently on the mouth. "Let's get married this weekend, Val," he urged. She was unable to speak, and he patted her behind before releasing her and putting himself to rights. "Get yourself together while I go out front and pretend I'm measuring the pipes." He pulled a tape measure from his pocket and went out the door.

Shakily she made herself presentable, almost falling again while struggling back into her girdle. Fortunately her lipstick was the non-smear type. She patted at her hair with her hands.

Mark came back into the small room with the metal tape measure in his hands. He showed her an extended section of it. "That's how much you just had up your sweet cunt," he told her softly.

"S-stop it!" she stammered faintly. She wet her dry lips with her tongue. "Do I—do I look all right?"

"Beautiful," he said fervently. "Beautiful."

She hardly remembered leaving the space behind the organ. Outside, in the more brightly lighted choir loft, Mark talked rapidly in an undertone and waved his arms about in large circles. He bowed low in silent thanks and then descended the loft steps. Valerie's assistant silently handed her the baton, and incredibly, she found herself mechanically conducting the choir while a small, slow trickle of moisture ran down the inside of her right thigh.

She and Mark weren't married that weekend, but never for an instant after that tumultuous few moments did Valerie doubt that she would indeed marry this forceful man. And never for a moment had she regretted it.

Sitting on the chaise longue, Valerie sighed, recalling it all. Mark had taken her measure and never removed his finger from the button ever since. And you love it, she told herself. Admit it. You love it.

She forced herself upright and into reluctant motion again. She went out into the kitchen and put on the coffee, opened the refrigerator door and decided she didn't want anything else, and sat down at the table. She had a steaming cup when it was ready, then went back upstairs. She made the bed and straightened up the bedroom, then started for the bath and her shower. She turned at the quick pad-pad of bare feet in the hallway.

A pajamaed Penny entered the bedroom, still rosy from sleep. The girl's shining black hair stood spikily over half her small head like a rakish halo, and her usual happy-go-lucky expression was sweetly serious. "Hi, mother." she said almost shyly. "I wondered—that is—are you still mad at me?" The final words tumbled out in a rush.

"Of course not, darling," Valerie said warmly. She held out her opened arms, and her youngest daughter sprinted across the intervening space between and flung herself into them, her sturdily fleshed, sleep-warmed young body moving Valerie backward a step. Valerie hugged her tightly, then dropped a hand and stroked Penny's pajama-clad bottom. "Any spank-marks, dear?" she asked lightly.

"I didn't look this morning," Penny admitted. She moved back a step, turned around, skinned down her pajama-bottoms, and presented her gleaming white backside for her mother's inspection. Valerie stared at the plump, wide-spanned, milk-white hind cheeks she had last seen galloping in scarlet agitation on Mark's knees. "How does it look?" the girl inquired.

"Unblemished," Valerie assured her. She sighed as Penny pulled up the pajama-bottoms. "You really don't have a fifteen-year-old-looking bottom, dear."

"That's what the boys say," Penny giggled.

Valerie smiled involuntarily, but cautionary maxims trembled at the tip of her tongue. She checked them momentarily. She knew that Penny, an indifferent scholar in contrast to Ethel's quick-minded absorption of lessons, had recently had her school horizons brightened immeasurably by her sudden discovery of boys. Valerie felt a sympathetic ache as she considered her daughter's bright-eyed inexperience. The greatest truism in the world seemed to be that the older generation couldn't live the younger's mistakes for them.

"Mother?" Penny said on an inquiring note.

"Yes, dear?"

"May I ask you a question? About—about yesterday?"

"Certainly," Valerie said steadily although she felt she knew what was coming. "Ask away."

Her brown-eyed daughter's young face had seldom looked more serious. "Why didn't you tell me about what men and women did so I wouldn't have been so—so surprised? I mean that it made you and Mark feel so good and wasn't—wasn't nasty like the girls make it sound?"

"Let's sit on the bed for a moment," Valerie suggested. They sat down side by side and Valerie slipped an arm around Penny's waist. "Now, darling," she began, "I probably should have told you, except that a parent is always afraid that if she makes something sexual sound too attractive, her little girl is likely to rush right out and try it with the first boy who comes down the street."

"And have a baby?" Penny smiled.

"Exactly. We're living in a permissive age, but society isn't prepared yet to be that permissive to the female of the species."

"I know three girls at school who are pregnant now," Penny said casually.

49

The remark jolted Valerie, but she tried not to show it. "It's certainly unfortunate that they are, because it can change their whole lives before they are able to make any decisions themselves."

Penny sat silently for a moment. "I guess what I really want to ask you, mother." she resumed, "is if you think it will be as nice for me when I'm married as it is for you and Mark?"

Valerie hesitated. "If you find someone as nice as Mark," she qualified the remark she had been about to make. "You're a little young to be thinking about it this soon, dear, but in a couple of years each boy you meet you should put through a screening process. You should ask yourself is this the boy with whom I want to live for the rest of my life? See his face on the next pillow every morning? Raise his babies? Minister to his ego as well as his sex drives? Wash his underwear? Sideline many of your own preferences in favor of his?"

Penny was listening intently. "But if—" "Let me say one more thing, darling, and then you can ask what you like." Valerie paused to marshal her thoughts. "All parents live for their children, Penny, but they must also live for each other. Children overlook the fact that parents were together before there were children, and in the normal course of events they will be together long after the children have gone off to school or in marriage. If the parents don't maintain their own intimacy, they have nothing left when their families are gone. Do you understand what I'm trying to say?" "I think so, mother." "Then what did you want to say?" Penny fastened her serious-looking brown eyes upon Valerie's. "But how can I tell when it's the right boy, mother?"

Valerie tightened the arm around her daughter's roly-poly waist. "If I had the answer to that, dear," she said with a little laugh, "I'd be a millionairess. Unfortunately we females are made so that we respond to all boys in some degree. The trick is the business of finding the boy who turns our constant sexual spark into a steady flame."

Valerie turned her head so that her face was inches from her daughter's. "At a party, Penny, two or three different boys might do this in a kissing game—" She pressed her lips upon her daughter's, gently at first, then more persistently. She darted her tongue between Penny's lips, searching out Penny's tongue and probing the girl's warm mouth. "And this, if you permit it," Valerie continued, breaking the mouth contact momentarily while she unbuttoned the two top buttons on Penny's pajama jacket.

Valerie resumed the kiss while her hand slipped inside the gaping jacket and cupped a warm, soft, bare breast. A shiver rippled through Penny's chubby flesh. Valerie cuddled the breast, playing with the nipple until its rosy peak stiffened in her palm. Penny whimpered softly although Valerie's mouth was once again fused upon her own. Valerie fondled her daughter's bare bubby which seemed to grow larger in her palm.

"Or this—" Valerie said, breaking off the mouth contact again as she undid the girl's pajama jacket entirely. Valerie lowered her head and plunged her mouth upon Penny's hardened pink nipple, licking at it and sucking it. Her daughter's knees jerked abruptly, but Valerie lipped whole portions of the tip-tilted full breast into her mouth and worked it around inside.

"Ooooooooooo!" Penny breathed.

Valerie dropped a hand upon the girl's pajama-clad thigh and speedily moved it to her thinly protected crotch, damp to the touch. Valerie traced the outline of the girl's chubby-lipped sex-furrow and then probed lightly at the squirming girlish cunt-hole while electric shocks ravaged her daughter's flesh as Valerie's mouth teased the round breast.

"Ohhhhhhhh, m-mother!" Penny gasped.

Valerie released her thoroughly titillated mouth-prisoner and sat up. Her hand still rested between Penny's thighs, but slackly. "Almost any boy can make you feel like that if you give him the opportunity, darling," she said soberly. "That's why it's so important to try to be sure it's the right boy before you let him."

Penny lowered her head upon Valerie's shoulder where her rapid breathing tickled Valerie's neck. "But how can you *t-tell,* mother? If it all feels so good?"

"Judgment is involved, dear," Valerie said. "But I think you can see now that the judgment needs to be applied before the situation becomes that critical."

"Boy, I'll say so," Penny murmured, then kissed her mother's neck. "Why does my stomach hurt now?"

"Because I was a pig and got you all stirred up without giving you any real relief," Valerie answered. She looked at the top of her daughter's shiningly black-haired head on her shoulder, started to say something, hesitated, then started again. "Penny—" she began, then paused.

Penny raised her brown eyes to Valerie's. "Yes, mother?"

Valerie put second thoughts aside. "Let's be naughty, dear," she said briskly. "Run over and lock the bedroom door."

Startled, Penny gazed at her mother questioningly for a second, then smiled delightedly. The girl slipped from the bed and trotted to the door which she locked. Valerie rose and removed her robe and gossamer nightgown. Penny returned to the bed and eyed her mother's womanly, full-curved nudity standing beside it. "Gee, mother," the girl sighed, "you have the most beautiful behind. No wonder Mark likes to play with it." Her voice was hushed. "What are we going to do?"

"Play," Valerie answered. "Skin out of your jammies, dear." When Penny complied, Valerie took her daughter's plumply dimpled nakedness into her arms. Their bare bellies rubbed gently, and Valerie brushed her own large breasts against Penny's smaller ones. Her hands fondled Penny's firm-fleshed but yielding hind cheeks, and after a moment Penny's hands came down and timidly stroked her mother's agreeably spacious broad-gauged nude seat. "Anything you like, dear," Valerie murmured against Penny's ear. "Do anything you like."

"Can I ask you a question first?"

"Ask away."

"When you're on your back, like—like yesterday, and Mark is on top of you, don't you feel squashed?"

"Here," Valerie said, taking her daughter's arm and moving her toward the bed. "Stretch out. On your back." Valerie advanced on her knees across the bed, spread Penny's round thighs, and lowered her own weight upon her daughter until the two rounded stomachs flowed together. "There. Do you feel squashed?"

"No," Penny said in a surprised tone. Valerie wriggled slightly on her daughter's soft body until she felt her own blond body-hair rubbing against Penny's thick-curled black moss. "Ooooh, boy!" the girl exclaimed. "Our pussies are touching, mother!"

"I want to show you something about your pussy," Valerie said, raising herself from Penny's body and then sitting beside her. "Lift up your legs, darling, and keep them apart."

Valerie fingered the disclosed pouting-lipped pink incision in its black-haired, cloistered retreat while Penny's upraised legs quivered. Valerie moved closer again between the parted thighs while she searched out her daughter's humid cuntal orifice with a fingertip and inserted it gently. She worked the fingertip back and forth and around and around, and it slipped in farther. "Does it hurt, dear?" she asked.

"Not—really," Penny answered in a strained voice. "Mother, I'm afraid I'm going to pee!"

"You won't," Valerie said confidently. "Just relax, dear."

She wormed her finger still farther inside Penny's clinging sheath until her knuckles widened the pouting moist lips and her fingertip fetched up against a resisting membrane. Penny flinched, and Valerie withdrew the finger. "That's your hymen, dear," she said quietly. "Your maidenhead, which you'll have until the first time a boy puts his prick into you. It usually hurts the first time, but seldom after that."

"They told us about it in school, but I never really knew where it was," Penny murmured. "And I hate to ask questions when everyone seems to know so much except me."

"The other girls probably have very little more knowledge than you, if that," Valerie returned. "That's how a girl gets into trouble later by not asking questions when she has a chance."

"Well, I know a boy's thing makes babies in a girl," Penny said defensively. She raised her head to see Valerie's face. "Will everything Mark did to you yesterday make a baby in you, mother?"

"It's entirely possible, Penny," Valerie answered, and was surprised at how much she welcomed the thought. "I'm not on the Pill."

"Some of the girls at school are," Penny said. "They sneak their mothers'. One girl's mother gives her her own bottle. Gee, wouldn't it be nice to have a little baby here at home?"

Her tone was so wistful that Valerie laughed. "Just so you leave it to me to have it." she warned with a playful

54

spank upon an upraised, dimpled hind cheek. "Now let me show you something else."

She reached in between Penny's widened legs and separated with two fingers the upper range of the girl's folded-together salmon fissure until the tiny pink-budded clitoris appeared. Valerie massaged it with the forefinger of her other hand, lightly at first and then with increasing pressure. Penny's breath whistled and her round bottom climbed from the bed. "Ohhhhhhh, mother!" she cried out. Her face turned scarlet and her legs strained upward. "Mother! I'm—oooh!—you're—aieee!—Mother! I'm—ohhhhhhhhhh-h-h!"

Valerie waited until the fluttering spasms and aftermath sighs had subsided, then touched her daughter's sex-flesh again to verify additional lubrication. "Surely you've felt that before, Penny?" she asked.

"Only when I turn over on my stomach and rub myself," Penny said, then blushed at the admission. "And I can't make it happen every time." She looked at her mother curiously. "Is that what you like so much when Mark—when Mark goes to bed with you?"

"That's part of it," Valerie said. "And it's best with a man like Mark. A strong man who knows how to give pleasure to a woman. Wait here a moment."

She went into the master bedroom's bathroom and soaked a washcloth in warm water, then returned with it and a hand towel to the bedroom. She washed Penny's oozing coral-colored sex-crevice gently while the girl wriggled uneasily, then patted it dry. She wanted Penny to feel clean for what came next. "You make me feel like a four-year-old, mother," the girl protested.

"You had the fattest little slit I've ever seen on a four-year-old," Valerie told her calmly. "All my girl friends used to take turns kissing it."

"Mother!"

"It's true. Whenever they dropped into the kitchen and I was bathing you." Valerie wadded up the washcloth inside the towel and discarded both on the floor. She moved in between Penny's legs again, still widened but resting laxly on the bed. Valerie tapped a thigh. "Lift them up, dear."

Obediently Penny elevated her marble-white chubby thighs. Valerie sank down upon the girl until she was breathing warmly upon Penny's jet-black silken fleece, the rose-hued protective cunt-lips right under her mouth. She darted her tongue along the yielding flesh-fissure, then probed with it. "Oooooooooooh!" Penny squealed. "Ohhhhhhhhh, m-mother!"

Valerie licked and tongued the fresh-smelling young cunt, her own mounting excitement creating a sympathetic moistness between her own tightly clenched thighs. Penny's legs clamped around Valerie's head as Valerie took quick, nipping mouthfuls of her daughter's pouting pussy and worried it. "Ohhhhhhhhh!" the girl gasped in exquisite delight as the fiery tongue wriggled into her hole and thrust forcefully up her sex-channel. "Oooooooooooh!"

Valerie raised her head slightly and worked her mouth over the girl's dewy chasm until the protective lips parted and she flirted with Penny's clitoris with the tip of her tongue. Penny's plump buttock-flesh quivered in her zestful agitation, and Valerie grazed the clit-bud with her teeth. "Aieeeeeeee!" Penny keened, and her stomach began jerking. "I'm—I'm—Ohh! I'm—" The girl couldn't form a sentence between exhilarated cunt-clutching orgasmic tremors. "Ohhh-h-h-h-h!" she moaned softly in an expiring sigh as her legs slackened.

Valerie tongued Penny's girlish spend from her lips as the girl raised her head. "Did you ever do that with Ethel, mother?" she wanted to know.

"Never," Valerie said firmly.

"Why not?"

Valerie hesitated. "I shouldn't say this, probably, but I never feel I can trust Ethel. About things like this, I mean. I just believe she'd try to turn it to her own advantage. Whereas you, you little dumpling—" Valerie squeezed a round breast lightly, "It's our special secret, isn't it?"

"Oh, yes," Penny confirmed eagerly. The girl scrambled to her knees. "Let me do you like that, mother. I want to try it."

"All right," Valerie agreed. "But it's tiring on the neck in that position until you've had a little practice. I'll move to the edge of the bed and you kneel between my legs."

They made the necessary arrangements, and Valerie went down on her back and raised her parted legs. Penny gazed with awe at her mother's upthrust ragged-lipped stout-looking soft pussy in its golden-haired whorl before lowering her young face upon the target. The girl licked experimentally at Valerie's cunt-hole, then raised her head to test the residue on her tongue. "You taste—funny, mother," she pronounced.

"You'll learn to love it dear," Valerie said dreamily.

Penny plunged her mouth firmly upon her mother's yielding sex-spot again and did her best to emulate her teacher. Valerie smiled tolerantly for a moment at the passionately amateurish efforts, then her smile faded as the hard-working young lips and mouth ignited her. Her hips moved upward subtly, then forcibly. She reached downward to seize her daughter's dark head and hold it tightly between her own legs. Her breath caught in her throat as she sought to speak. "That's—wonderful, Penny, delightful—Ohhh, you dear!—delight—ohhh! You darling! You darLINNNNNG! Ohhhh, I'm—I'm coming!"

Her hips bucked furiously as she came, and it was another moment before she released her daughter's head pinioned between her thighs. Penny rubbed at her ears gently. "Boy, you really take hold, mother, don't you?" she said in half-protestation. Then she smiled. "But I did you, didn't I?"

"You certainly did," Valerie said. "Come here and let me show you a refinement."

She arranged the girl over her own body so that Penny's head was above Valerie's groin and Penny's wide-spreading young buttocks were over her mother's face. Valerie reached up and slapped a glistening globe. "Go to work down there," she said as she pressed with her hands until her daughter's hairy little pussy descended upon her mouth. As she aimed her tongue at it Valerie could feel Penny's quick tongue employed down below.

For five minutes the only sound in the bedroom was the soft-slurping tongues as they worked for a moment, rested, then busied themselves again. When Valerie was sure neither of them was going to come again, she called a halt. Penny climbed off her, switched ends, and snuggled herself into Valerie's arms. "Gee, mother," she sighed, "You know all kinds of games, don't you?" The tip of her tongue cleansed her greasy lips. "It does taste better." She looked at Valerie questioningly. "What else can we do?"

"Nothing, you little glutton," Valerie laughed. "For now," she amended it upon seeing Penny's disappointed expression. "Your sister is due home shortly from her tennis lesson. We both have to get dressed."

Penny stretched in catlike contentment, rubbing her taut-nippled breasts against her mother's elegantly sculptured large bosom. "I think I'm jealous, mother," the girl announced. "You can do this, and then you have Mark, too. Gee, when we were in the closet and his enormous thing was going in and out of your pussy like a—like a jackhammer, I got so wet I could hardly stand myself."

"In about two or three years we'll find you a boy, dear," Valerie promised. "A boy as nice as Mark." She pinched a soft thigh. "Scoot, now and remember, mum's the word."

"Mum's the word," Penny echoed with a giggle.

The girl climbed from the bed, slipped into her pajamas, went to the door and unlocked it, and pitter-patted down the hallway.

CHAPTER IV

"Were you serious at the motel when you spoke about bringing Neal home from military school to complete the school year with the girls at the local high school?" Mark asked Valerie that night. They were again seated upon the chaise longue in front of the fireplace.

"Certainly I was serious," Valerie returned warmly. "I hate thinking of Neal in that—that spartan atmosphere when he could be enjoying family life here with us."

"Well, if you don't see any complications, I'll call the school's commandant in the morning and make the arrangements," Mark said. He patted Valerie's hand. "The more I think about it, the more I feel you have the right idea."

"That's settled, then," Valerie said. "You arrange for his transcript to be transferred, and I'll speak to James Rollins, the principal, about Neal's enrolling."

"And you'd better speak to the girls," Mark added. "I still have an uneasy feeling they might consider it an invasion of privacy."

"Not a chance," Valerie declared confidently. "They both liked him when he visited us. Penny followed him around like a puppy." She moved closer to Mark. The morning's activities with Penny had left her excited but essentially unslaked, It was after midnight, and the house was quiet. She unzipped Mark's trousers and fumbled in his shorts until she brought out his limp prick which she balanced on her palm. "Poor little wizened old man," she mourned sorrowfully, and dropped her bright-gold head upon the shriveled cock.

She licked the tip delicately, and almost immediately there was a stirring in her husband's flesh. The purple head grew taut as the prick expanded and lengthened. Valerie took it in her mouth and sucked steadily at the same

61

time she whisked her tongue along the vein underneath. A muscle in Mark's thigh jumped and his hands came down and rested on his wife's head. Valerie swirled her tongue around the rapidly stiffening prong and moved her mouth back and forth on it as it crowded her throat.

"Don't waste it!" Mark said hoarsely. "Get your clothes off!"

They both undressed quickly, and Mark seated himself again and drew Valerie down upon his lap so that her wide, soft, bare bottom was prodded by the rampant prick under her. Mark kissed her lingeringly while he played with her breasts, then with her protruding scarlet nipples. His hand dropped down and played with her navel as shivers puckered Valerie's flesh, then with the round bowl of her velvety stomach and the fleecy white-gold hair on her prominent mound. By the time he dipped a finger into her musky treasure-trove, the inner walls of Valerie's invaded cunt were contracting spasmodically and bedewing the invader. She screwed herself down harder on the finger while beneath her the surging cock jabbed at her soft under-parts.

"You've got to have the hottest cunt in the country," Mark said huskily. "I've never found you dry." He eased Valerie from his lap onto her back on the chaise, then spread and widened her legs as he moved in between them. He picked up her legs and doubled them back until her uplifted, pouting-lipped, pink pussy was in range of his long, rigid cock.

Valerie relaxed on her back and felt the delicious initial bumping of the blunt-headed cock against her soft-lipped incision. The big prick probed, retreated, advanced, then lodged itself suddenly as she gulped at the quick distention within her quivering pussy. "Ohhhhhhh-h-h-h!" she moaned feebly as the invasion continued.

"M-Mark!"

He worked his hard gristle into her slowly, backing off frequently and making quick little jabbing runs into Valerie's quiff that brought her legs up from the chaise involuntarily. Each time the blunt head dived more deeply, and Valerie's breath whistled. "Ohhh, God!" she gasped. "It's—*enormous*—tonight!"

She came before Mark was fully into her, in a flurry of stomach-jerking spasms and cunt-contracting writhings that had her whimpering loudly. Mark worked his stout staff into his wife's newly lubricated channel up to the hilt, then rested for a moment until her body agitation died away. When he began to move on her, she at once became vocal again.

"Ahh! Ahh! Ahhh!" Valerie enunciated clearly as Mark's big prick plunged into her repeatedly. She raised her legs and wrapped them around her husband's back, exposing her uplifted big bottom with the long white cock pistoning in and out of her greasy-shiny receptacle. "Ooooooh! Mark! Ohhhhhh! What a—gorgeous—fuck! Ahhhhh! Fuck me! Fuck me—*hard*—you lovely—fuzzy bear!" Her hands raced over the hard hirsute body pinning her to the chaise.

A shadow moved on the wall closest to them, but in the throes of passion neither noticed it. On the stairway, Ethel, clad in her nightgown, watched with mingled emotions the tremendous fucking being given to her mother by her stepfather. A touch of fastidious disgust at the seemingly awkward naked bodies in their sweaty labors was overwhelmed by a feeling of envy at Valerie's manifest rapture at what Mark's fierce sex-engine was doing to her all-engulfing cunt. Ethel stared from the stairway, fascinated, at the white bodies showcased against the darker.

"Ohhh! Ohhhh! M-Mark!" Ethel heard her mother cry out shrilly as Mark's huge prick continued to bury itself in her oozing trench. "I'm—coming, Mark! Mark! Ooooooooooh, I'm—*coining!*"

Her mother's soft flesh seemed convulsed as it churned itself madly on the spike of Mark's penetration of it, and Ethel hardly dared blink for fear of missing something as Mark's hands slid beneath his wife's perspiring buttocks and pulled her up more tightly against him as he attacked the yielding flesh beneath him with seemingly mindless force. Ethel winced at each resounding impact, but Valerie's hands fluttered along her husband's back, patting, fondling, and soothing. She was holding him tightly to her when Mark boiled over and shot a load into her that seemed to go on and on, then rested laxly upon her with a sigh that seemed to the watching Ethel to come from the core of his being.

She remained on the stairway until the two entwined figures separated, then crept noiselessly back up the stairs and went into her bedroom. She closed the door all but a crack, then stood with her eyes focused on the top of the stairway. In minutes she heard the murmur of voices as her mother and stepfather climbed the stairs. Valerie appeared first, naked, carrying her clothing. Then Mark was there suddenly beside her, also nude. Ethel could even see the frictionized red marks on her mother's lower belly and the uncommon redness of her stepfather's shrunken penis.

Valerie and Mark paused outside their bedroom door for a long, arms-wrapped-around-each-other kiss. Then they disappeared inside, and the door closed. Ethel stood staring down the hallway for a moment, disappointed that the show was over. Then she closed her own door, moved across the room to her dressing table, and turned on its light. In the sudden illumination she pulled her nightgown up and captured it under her armpits while she studied her nudity in the lighted mirror.

She examined carefully the quick swell of her firm-thrusting breasts with ruby teats set in dark areolas, the smooth sweep of her navel-dimpled belly as it plunged into the bronze-haired conjuncture of her round white thighs. She nodded her head, finally, and let the nightgown descend.

Ethel Walker had made up her mind.

She turned out the light and went to bed, to toss and turn for a long time as visions of Valerie's and Mark's sex-blended naked bodies disturbed her peace of mind.

She rose in the morning with a plan of action fully formed. It was the day for Valerie's bridge luncheon, removing one possible source of conflict. Penny's activities were usually scorned by Ethel unless they threatened to intrude upon the older sister's plans. Besides, what Ethel planned for the day had nothing to do with after-school programs.

Before donning underwear after her shower she went to her closet and examined the dresses inside. She chose one in shining black knitted terrycloth of 100-percent rayon with side slits, back zipper, and a white-daisy sash tie in front to relieve its starkness. It was short enough to be worn with pants if desired, but Ethel had no intention of concealing her good-looking legs. Instead, she donned her sheerest pantyhose in a misty gentian-violet hue.

On impulse she ignored her bra before slipping the dress over her auburn hair. The slinky material of the dress clung to her jutting breasts, teasing the nipples until they stiffened. She waited until the mini-erections died away before going down to breakfast, braced against her mother's queries about her finery. Valerie, however, immersed in thoughts of Neal's homecoming, didn't notice. Penny eyed her sister's fine feathers askance, but to Ethel's relief made no comment.

The older sister avoided her mother until it was time to leave for school. She sat through her first two periods tensely, mental images tumbling through her mind to the distraction of all learning capability. Then she went to the school nurse and got herself excused for the balance of the day for non-existent period cramps.

She walked two blocks from school, then took a cab. At fifteen minutes before noon she showed up at Mark Walker's office, which took in the entire third floor of the Cardwell Building and made herself known to the receptionist. "Your daughter is here to see you, Mr. Walker," the receptionist announced over the intercom.

Ethel just had time to be impressed with the seemingly endless desks stretching away into the distance and the numerous semi-private cubicles when a door opened at the end of the room's first section and Mark appeared in it. Ethel walked toward him as casually as she could manage. "Hi," she said in a voice she strove to make just as casual. "I thought you might like to take me to lunch today."

One look at the slinky dress and the violet-gentian pantyhose and Mark had the entire picture. He had been expecting Ethel to make a move, and he was delighted with her ingenuity although he kept his expression bland. "Of course," he said smoothly, standing aside to permit the girl to enter his private office. "But we can have a better lunch right here without bothering to go out. I'll have something sent up from next door."

Ethel was staring abstractedly around the room, which was furnished more like a living room than an office except for Mark's large desk and swivel chair. The carpeting was deep pile, and tasteful abstractions were on the walls. The remainder of the furniture was Victorian in style, and the room's indirect lighting glinted upon its richly polished dark wood.

"Sit down, sit down," Mark said genially, then bent over the intercom on his desk. He ordered ham-and-turkey plates with potato salad, toasted English muffins, apple pie with cheese, and iced tea. As an afterthought he ordered a bottle of rose wine. "Sound all right?" he asked as Ethel sank into a chair near his desk. The chair tilted from front to back so precipitously that Ethel felt sure her short skirt had risen to a point almost disclosing the crotch of her pantyhose, and she kept her thighs clenched self-consciously.

Mark chatted easily about inconsequential items as a girl came in from the outer office and set a table for two in one corner, complete with napkins, silverware, and wine glasses. A waiter appeared with two large trays, and Mark steered Ethel to the table with a hand on her elbow when the luncheon repast was ready. Ethel sat down almost in a daze at so much unexpected elegance while Mark poured her a half-glass of the wine.

"You—I had no idea you employed so many people," Ethel said to make conversation that was coming hard for her. She could feel the maleness radiating from her luncheon companion, and it confused her.

"You mean all the girls?" Mark smiled. "I like pretty girls, or maybe you'd noticed already?" Ethel felt herself blushing despite her best effort to match her host's nonchalance. Mark raised his glass and waited until the girl followed suit. "To our mutual enjoyment of the pleasant occasion," he toasted, and Ethel's color rose again as she sipped at her wine.

The food was delicious, and she ate heartily. Mark continued to speak wittily on various subjects, and despite her mother's previously unsuspected bodily sophistication, Ethel marveled anew that she had been able to capture this sophisticated man. When they finished, the waiter came back and cleared the table and the same girl, a striking redhead, restored the corner to its semi-officelike appearance.

When the room was empty except for himself and Ethel, Mark sat down at his desk momentarily. "No calls until I let you know," he informed the receptionist and his private secretary over the intercom at the same time he kneed a switch on the underside of his desk that locked his office door. He looked at Ethel. "Would you like to see the rest of my setup here?"

"The rest?" she echoed.

Mark rose from his desk and went to one wall where he punched the bottom frame of a painting. A hidden door swung open, disclosing to Ethel's startled eyes a miniature bedroom and bathroom, both exquisitely furnished in the best of taste. "We can be more comfortable in there, don't you think?" Mark proposed.

"N-no," Ethel said instinctively. She realized she was losing entirely whatever frail grip she had had on the situation.

Mark smiled at her benignly. "Look, Ethel," he said softly. "We both know why you're here. You thought I'd take you out to lunch, and you'd turn on the girlish charm, and we'd do it again, and you'd do it again, and sooner or later we'd end up in the sack together." His smile widened. "So why bother with the buildup? Just walk inside there and we'll roadtest the product." His smile turned taunting. "Or are you going to chicken out?"

Ethel had never felt more gauche or less sophisticated. She knew she had been outmaneuvered, and she didn't know how to regain the lost ground. Mark strolled to her casually, put his arms around her, and kissed her hard, the hard male lips crushing Ethel's slightly parted ones. A quick tongue darted into her mouth, stirring her despite her best effort at repressing her arousal. Mark broke off the kiss and stared down at her from his superior height although she was a tall girl. "Let's go inside and I'll try your cunt on my prick for size," he said. Through the thin stuff of her dress he fondled an un-brassiered breast. "Hmmmmm, came ready, did you?"

He led her into the bedroom, and Ethel allowed herself to be shepherded like a sleepwalker. Overpowering waves of masculinity flowed from Mark Walker, and she felt as helpless as the time when he took her panties down and spanked her. "Strip," Mark told her, and proceeded to remove his own jacket, tie, and shirt.

Ethel knew her bluff had been called, if it indeed had been a bluff; at the moment she could be sure only that she wasn't going to let herself appear chicken in the eyes of this man. She removed her dress and hung it carefully over the back of a chair, then stood hesitant as Mark stooped and removed his shoes. Beneath her slip Ethel had on only her pantyhose, and she shrank from the feeling of nudity she knew would follow removal of the slip.

Again Mark anticipated her reaction. He unbuckled his belt and unzipped his trousers, then stepped out of them. Immediately he drew down his shorts and cast them aside. Ethel looked at the bunched maleness of his groin with his white prick and hairy balls beneath his undershirt, and looked away. Her throat felt dry.

Mark took hold of the slip and worked it off over Ethel's head. Almost negligently he squeezed a firm but pliant buttock in its gossamer covering, then moved his hand around in front and stroked Ethel's mossy mound through the pantyhose. She flinched, and he smiled. "Virgin?" he asked easily.

"Y-yes," she whispered.

He smacked his lips deliberately. "I haven't had an honest-to-God cherry in a hundred years, Ethel."

"I'll—I'll probably bleed like a stuck pig," she said desperately. "Your—your penis is so big."

He began to draw the elasticized waist of the pantyhose down over her sleek white buttocks. "Easy is as easy does," he said soothingly, stripping the clinging, undergarment from her completely. He turned her around to admire her rear view. "Like I tell your ma, Ethel, you've got ass you haven't used yet." He stroked the warm, malleable globes that developed goose-bumps at his touch, then

69

plunged his hand deeply into her buttock-crevice and cupped her pussy on his palm. Ethel gave a little jump as Mark's voice deepened. "It's about time you decided to use this for something more than to piss through, Ethel."

Both his hand and his words were exciting the girl, A volatile flame seemed to flicker from her pussy-lips being played with by the big hand well up into her stomach. A touch on the back of the thigh caused her to look around. The previously limp cock was standing forth erectly, jabbing at her bare leg. Ethel shivered at the sight of the massive rigidity.

As though sensing her fear, Mark sat down on the bed with Ethel on his lap. He kissed her breasts and tongued the cranberry-hued nipples. He played with her belly and shifted her so he could play with her bottom. And then he fused his mouth on hers again while he slipped a finger into her tight cunt-hole after teasing the soft curls adorning her sweetly curved lower abdomen.

She was still trembling, but with a difference they both felt. A wild surge of sensation was boiling up in Ethel's sensitive grotto, overwhelming her fear. Mark frigged her steadily with a curved finger until her pussy-lips turned moist and her breath was coming in quick sighs. He kissed her mouth, her breasts, and the nape of her neck, and Ethel writhed on his lap as she felt herself getting wetter than she had ever been in her life.

"Run into the bathroom and get a towel," Mark told her.

She rose at once and did so, eager now to get on with her own defloration. "Don't mind if I yell," she said to Mark when she returned to the bed and handed him the towel. "Mother says I'm an awful baby when I'm hurt." For the first time she gathered the courage to reach down and take his elongated prick in her hand, her eyes widening at the combined soft-hard feel of the blood-engorged stout shaft. "Oooooooh, it will *never* go in!" she said in despair. "My pussy aches just looking at it."

He spread the towel on the bed, then picked her up by the waist and sat her down with her shining-white behind upon it. He arranged her legs and lowered himself upon her shrinking stomach until his aroused prick rested on her red-gold fleece. Then he tucked it underneath so that with each movement it scraped the length of her coral-pink sex-fissure.

Ethel sprawled on her back uneasily with her eyes closed, waiting for the searing pain she had dreaded ever since at ten an older girl had explained importantly what happened when a boy put his thing into a girl. But Mark's finger moved in alongside his meaty shaft and once again entered her cunt-hole, frigging the girl slowly at first and then faster as her legs began to quiver. Internal moistness dampened the frigging finger as Ethel's juices were again stirred.

The girl tightened up again from her momentarily relaxed love affair with the probing finger when she felt Mark replace his knees and line the tip of his hard cock up with her shrinking pussy-lips. The blunt head bored into her slightly, wiggled from side to side, backed off, then advanced again.

"How's it going?" Mark Walker asked his step-daughter.

"It's softer—than your finger!" Ethel gasped. "But oooooh, it's *stretching* me!"

With infinite patience he moved in and out of the tight sheath in the smallest of increments, gradually enlarging his prick-hold on the virgin cunt. Twice he pulled out entirely and rubbed saliva all over his reddened prong, then moved back to the fray as Ethel's thighs tensed apprehensively. Finally he ended up drawing an extra wince from the

71

girl as the blunt head of his straining prick encountered a fibrous obstruction.

Mark reached down and took hold of Ethel's smoothly sculptured nude hind cheeks in both hands, kneading and massaging the soft flesh. "You've got the prettiest bare ass a girl could ever hope to have her boy friend unveil on the back seat of a car," he told her, attempting to distract her with his words as much as with his manipulation of her silken, yielding behind. "I don't know when I've seen—"

When he started the second sentence, Mark pulled Ethel up tightly against himself at the same instant he bored into her with his prick. He smashed through her hymen and lodged in her fully while her body gave a great, convulsive leap.

"OWWWWWWWWWWWWWWW!!!." Ethel shrieked. "Ooooooh, it's burning! It's—*burning!* Ohhhhhh-h-h-h-h!"

Mark remained motionless on her belly, his long cock imbedded in the girl's raw-feeling cunt. Ethel's choked sobs of distress died away as her cunt sheath adjusted gradually to its sudden dilation. Mark clenched his buttock muscles and Ethel whimpered aloud at the feeling of prick-movement inside her, but there was no longer the same feeling of urgency in her voice.

Cautiously Mark began to move on her round stomach, raising and lowering his hips slightly. "Owwwww!" Ethel breathed, but again with no indication of impaled distress. She was so tight that his prick-head was throbbing, and he made no attempt to restrain his natural reaction. "Oooooh, what was *that?*" Ethel exclaimed, startled, as Mark's load of sperm traveled from his balls and deluged the girl's distended sheath.

"Shhhhh-h-h!" Mark murmured, relaxing on her belly again. The slight diminishment of his erection coupled with his copious discharge soothed Ethel's scraped-feeling inner walls.

When Mark began to move upon her again, a new note crept into the young voice.

"M-Mark?" she said uncertainly. "It's—your thing feels—funny—in me. It feels:—" She lost her voice in a high-pitched gasp as Mark settled down to plowing her garden. "Ohhh! I never—felt—oooooh—! It's so—big and so—*deep!* Ohhhhh!"

Mark had regained all of his original erection, but they were both well-lubricated now. He slanted in and out of Ethel's newly juicy pussy and the girl attempted uncoordinatedly awkward thrustings of her inexperienced hips. "Let me do it this time, baby," Mark said hoarsely in her ear. "You've got—forty years—to play—the whore."

But she didn't hear him. "Ohhhhhh!" she squealed almost in a falsetto as the big prick fucked her seething cunt. "Oooooh! Mark!" Her legs climbed his back, again awkwardly but eagerly ardent. Her floundering beneath him almost sent him into another orgasm, but he held off, determined to make her come so she would remember the experience as pleasurable.

He speared her bronze-haired doughnut in a steady rhythm, and her voice rose again, almost querulously. "Ohhhhh?" she got out in a questioning mew. Her slender thighs bucked from the excess of emotion radiating through her. "Ohhhh, Mark! I'm—oooh! Something's—*tickling!* Ohh! Ohh! Ohhh, Mark! Ohhhh-h-h-h!"

He could feel the unguided quick thrusting of her warm belly as orgasm overwhelmed her.

While her involuntary cunt-contractions were still nipping at his fleshy rod he splashed her again with a bountiful come, then pillowed his head on her firm young breasts.

Ethel raised her head questioningly when she felt him shrinking within her. "Is it—over?" she asked, nibbling at her lower lip. "I mean—there isn't any more?"

Despite himself he laughed. "You mean you want more?"

She blushed deeply. "Well, near the end there it was getting—well, wild!"

"Your finger never did that for you?"

She turned scarlet. "I don't know what you mean," she said stiffly.

"I mean when you played with yourself in bed nights."

She couldn't look him in the eye. "That's I—I'm—" She swallowed hard. "H-how did you know?" she whispered.

"Do you think you're the only one who can hide in closets?" he teased.

"Oooooooooh," she moaned, mortified.

He moved her hips on the towel. "Look," he said. She raised herself to do so. There were blood-and-semen stains on the thighs but surprisingly little blood on the towel. "Do you really think you had a maidenhead?"

"Well, I had *something* that you ripped in there!" she said vigorously. She flexed her thighs slowly. "Does my pussy ever feel tender!" She looked up at him with more of her natural ginger than at any time since he had put her on her back. "Was I better than mother?" she asked impudently.

"I ought to whale your ass," he said disgustedly. "Hardly got your cunt broken in and you're asking me to compare you to the best. If you ever get to be half the fuck your mother is, kiddo, you'll have put in a good day's work." He considered what he had said. "Make that a couple of years' work."

74

"I will be better, though," Ethel said confidently. "You wait and see." She put a hand on his arm as he started to move from the bed. "Why don't you put it into me from behind like you do with mother?"

His laugh that time was grudgingly unwilling. "Listen, girl, as it is you're going to walk bowlegged for two days. Get inside there and soak yourself in a hot tub, then-go home and tell Valerie you landed wrong on the sawhorse during gym at school. Otherwise you're going to find yourself trying to answer questions you won't want to answer."

"But we'll do it again?" she asked eagerly. "Ill be better next time. All I need is practice."

"Somehow I believe you, Ethel," he said slowly, "And you can be sure we'll do it again."

He shepherded her into the bathroom, then returned to his office, still naked, for his cigarettes. Back in the bedroom he picked up her scattered clothing and brought it into the bathroom to her. When she climbed from the tub, he swathed her in a fluffy towel and patted her dry. "How's the scene of the recent accident?" he inquired, trailing his fingers down over her damp body-curls to her pouting sex-gash.

"Sore," she said frankly. "But I don't mind." She lifted one leg and then the other. "It feels—it feels almost as though you forgot and left something in there."

"You're still stretched," he said tolerantly. "But you'll shrink." He watched her dress, aiming a paternal spank at a naked buttock just before it disappeared into her panty-hose. "Why'd you come here today? Couldn't you get yourself poked by anyone in school?"

"Of course I could," she said scornfully. "But you made mother feel so good I wanted it to be you. And I think I was right about it." She presented her back to him for her dress to be zipped up, and he obliged.

"Thanks for the compliment, sis," he said with less of his usual flippancy. "You're going to be a good fuck one of these days."

She beamed at him, then glanced toward his office. "Should I go now?"

"Not that way," he said. He went to his clothes and removed his key ring. He unlocked a door set flush with the wall inside the bedroom. "You'll find two doors locked on your side that you can let yourself through," he told her. "See you tonight."

"Aren't you clever fixing it so no one knows how long your—your guests stay?" Ethel said admiringly.

"Scoot," he said, but he was smiling. He watched her walk to the first locked door, his eyes on her thighs-apart gingerly stride. His smile widened as he closed the door on its invisible seam and locked it again. Things were right on schedule.

He showered and started to take fresh underwear from a bureau drawer, then stood in the bedroom, thinking. That tight little cunt had been a bit of all right, and it would be even better with no necessity for restraint in the future. Just thinking about it, his prick rose from between his thighs. Mark looked down at his heavy meat with the purple head emerging snakelike from the withdrawing foreskin. Damn, maybe he should have kept the girl a few minutes longer and backdoored her as she wanted.

There was an alternative, of course.

He waited another moment to be sure the erection was no false alarm, then left his fresh underwear in the bureau drawer and walked through the bedroom to his desk. He flipped the switch on the intercom that connected him with the secretarial pool. "Miss Rounseville," he said.

"Yes, Mr. Walker?" a feminine voice floated back.

"Dictation, please."

He released the office doorlock and went back into the bedroom. When the striking redhead who had set the luncheon table entered the office, Mark walked in from the bedroom, still naked. The girl's eyes widened. "Get your pants down, Lily, and your belly on the desk," Mark ordered. He had already decided that after Ethel's tight cunt he couldn't come off in a relaxed pussy. He approached his desk, kneed the lock on again, and removed a jar of vaseline from a drawer.

"Oh, please, Mark," the redhead pleaded with her skirt already waist high. "Not in my ass. Please."

"Definitely in your ass, Lily," Mark said curtly. "If you expect to continue working here."

Helplessly the redhead skinned down pink panties and gingerly lowered her belly upon the desk top. Mark approached her sleekly plump bare behind, obstructed only by garter belt tapes, and slathered vaseline in between her buttocks and inside her tight-puckered anus. Then he did the same for his rigid cock.

He paused to work the vaseline deeper into the girl's flinching rectum before removing his finger and applying the tip of his vaselined prick to her vaselined bottom-hole. He bucked experimentally a couple of times, and Lily's white bottom quivered. She moaned quietly as he began to penetrate her in earnest. Mark never cared how much noise the women he brought to the office made. With all the other money he'd spent getting the setup fixed up to his satisfaction, a little more for soundproofing had been a good investment.

He shoved harder as the head of his cock slipped inside the redhead's distended anus. He grunted and strained as his prick forced its way into the girl's buttery-feeling rectum. The feel of her soft flesh against his thighs excited him. Lily was crying openly as Mark began to plunge into her pain-wracked flesh.

"Where am I fucking you, Lily?" Mark asked sadistically.

"In—my—asshole," the redhead got out between sobs, knowing what he wanted.

It was over too quickly to really suit Mark. Before he was ready he felt the deep trembling in his loins, and then his hot sperm was gushing from his prick into Lily's palpitating clenched bottom-hole. Mark groaned aloud as he wrung out the last few drops into the quivering rectum, then pulled out of the girl with a sound like the slapping of his two palms together. A river of sperm ran from Lily's bunghole down her thighs, and she wiped frantically at herself with her hands to keep it from reaching her garter-belted stocking tops.

"Clean things up here," Mark said gruffly, and went back to the bathroom and the shower.

He was thinking that he had been saving Valerie's virgin asshole—so far as he knew, and he was sure he did—and he didn't really know why.

Perhaps it was time to do something about that tasty morsel.

CHAPTER V

Mark Walker rose late on Sunday morning. He showered leisurely after checking his watch. Valerie would be directing the choir, and the girls would be with her at church. Mark whistled cheerfully as he toweled himself off. They were picking Neal up at the airport that afternoon to complete the balance of his senior year at the local high school. Mark smiled at the thought. He found the idea interesting. Very interesting.

Again in this robe, Mark started for the stairs and the kitchen, a cup of steaming black coffee foremost in his mind. His attention was diverted suddenly as he passed the girls' bedrooms en route to the stairway and in Penny's room he saw the black flood of .her hair on the pillow. For some reason the younger sister hadn't gone to church.

Mark hesitated momentarily, then entered the bedroom. He hadn't been able to indulge his sybaritic tastes all these years by pussyfooting around. He sat down on the edge of the bed and considered the sleeping girl.

His weight on the springs created enough of a difference in her position that Penny stirred, yawned, knuckled her eyes, then opened them. She stared uncomprehendingly at Mark seated on her bed before she really focused upon him. "Are you ill, Penny?" Mark asked in pretended concern.

She shook her dark head in confusion. "I'm—no, I'm fine. I asked mother if I had to go, and she said not if I didn't want to attend. It's just—I'm afraid I'm not very religious. Or a very good Christian."

"I'm sure you're just as good a Christian as the average individual under the church roof this morning," Mark said drily.

A silence ensued which Mark was content to leave unbroken. He wanted the girl ever more conscious of his male presence so close to her pajamaed person. Of course Penny was young enough—still not sixteen—to be unaware, or partly unaware, of the implication of his presence in her bedroom, Mark thought.

When she spoke, she immediately proved it.

"I've never thanked you for letting me off so easily, Mark," she said shyly, using his name as he had insisted upon right after his marriage to Valerie. "Not spanking harder, I mean, when—when mother caught us in the closet, watching."

"It seemed criminal to really wallop such a pretty behind." Mark said solemnly. Penny blushed vividly, a rosy tide of color that enveloped her young features. "I don't recall when I've seen such a beautifully shaped bare bottom, Penny," Mark continued. He sighed deeply. "I'd love to see it again." Penny's high color increased as Mark forced her gaze meet his own. "Would you show it to me?"

The girl swallowed visibly. "You mean right now?" she whispered.

"Right now," Mark said cheerfully, and threw back the sheet and blanket. "Stand up, Penny."

His hand under her arm assisted her to her knees and then to her feet. He had no intention of waiting for her to make up her mind. Instead, he faced her away from him and drew the elasticized waist of the girl's pajama pants down over her chubby nude backside and well down her thighs. It was better this way. Afterward the girl could excuse herself by telling herself she really hadn't had anything to do with it.

Penny sucked in her breath sharply at her sudden exposure. One small hand instinctively sought to conceal a plump bare globe, but Mark gently removed the hand. He stared avidly at the sleekly protuberant hemispheres with a peach-fuzz tracing of hair starting at the dimple at the base of her spine and disappearing into the deep cleft separating her snowy gluteal region.

"Bend over, Penny," Mark said quietly.

"Oh, no!" she responded, still in a whisper.

"Bend over," he repeated.

After another few seconds' hesitation, she did so. Mark licked his lips unconsciously as he studied the plumped-out, thrust-back sweep of naked girl-flesh, bed-warmed and sweet-smelling. He cupped a nude, pearly-white haunch upon one palm and jiggled it lightly. Penny's breath rasped in her throat. Her bent-forward position had tightened her flesh until Mark could see a wisp of dark, fleecy body hair protruding backward through the girl's clenched thighs.

"You have a lovely bare behind, Penny," Mark assured her fervently. He stood up, and then stooped slightly so that he could kiss in turn each of the younger sister's disquieted portly spheres.

"Ooooooo!" Penny gasped upon a rising note. Her entire bottom quivered from her reaction to the warm lips pressed upon her intimate flesh. "Ohhhh-h, Mark!"

The feminine effluvia filled Mark's nostrils, and his penis rose massively beneath his robe. He kissed each bare hind cheek again, then applied his thumbs to the fullest portion of the lower hindquarters, widening the cheeks until the paler aureole of the girl's anus appeared, framed above and below by a wispy thread of body-hair deep in her crevice.

Mark advanced his face between the separated girlish fanny-cheeks until he could breathe heavily upon the newly exposed little buttonhole. Penny's thighs trembled, and goose bumps sprang up upon her downy flesh. "Mark!" she pleaded. "Ohh, Mark!"

He turned his face until he could penetrate more deeply the deliciously odorous furrow, then licked at the girl's shrinking asshole with the tip of his tongue.

81

"Oooooh!" Penny squealed in excited dismay. "Ooooooooooooh!!!"

Her wriggling bare buttocks bumped Mark's face, but he pursued his target steadily, thrusting his tongue sturdily at the contracted orifice. It was only when Penny's movements threatened to tear her body out of his hands entirely that he stopped his tonguing of her and stepped back. Penny squatted to pull her pajama trousers back up, and just before they enveloped her silky-skinned backside, Mark's palm spatted lightly upon each satiny rump-globe.

"Thank you, Penny," he said gravely, and left the bedroom. It was enough for the moment, and he wanted no post-mortems for the moment. The girl's rosily confused young face was proof enough that he'd made his point.

Mark took his rampant erection down to the kitchen and poured himself a cup of coffee after re-plugging in the percolator Valerie had left on the table. He drank a glass of orange juice, considered toast and decided against it, and had just decided to return upstairs and shave when the car drove into the yard with Valerie at the wheel and Ethel sitting beside her.

He sat at the table while mother and daughter entered the kitchen via the back door. Valerie was in white, Ethel in pastel blue. Mark's nostrils widened as he considered Valerie's full-bodied charms. The knowledge of the warm cunt beneath her Sunday-go-to-meeting clothes stirred his erection again.

"How are you, dear?" Valerie greeted him smilingly.

"Never better," he assured her, rising from the table. "Let's go upstairs. I have something to show you."

Valerie didn't misunderstand his meaning. She glanced quickly at her daughter who hadn't misunderstood, either. Mark saw that Ethel's mouth was set in a thin-lipped line. Jealous, he thought. Beautiful.

He put his arm around Valerie's waist and led her toward the stairs. He stopped once in mid-flight to kiss her warmly on her soft mouth, and her lips came alive beneath his. They entered their bedroom, and Mark closed the door. Silently he parted the front of his robe and showed his wife his erection.

"It's lovely, dear," she said, taking it in her hand and fondling it. "But I think Ethel knew what you meant."

"She's a big girl now," Mark said casually in the manner of a man with more important things on his mind. "Let me help you out of your things." He took her in his arms and patted her girdled croup. "Let's get the armorplate off this piece of machinery and put it to work."

Together they removed Valerie's dress and slip, unzipped her girdle, and tugged it down over her substantial hips and full thighs. Mark took her in his arms again and kissed her fiercely while his hands laved the area of bare skin on her back between her bra and panties. "Mark!" Valerie implored when he freed her lips again. "My panties are getting wet!"

Together they pulled down her panties over her already down-dropping stockings whose girdle-garters had disappeared. Mark dropped down on his knees and kissed the girdle-marks on the soft bowl of her belly, then turned her around and did the same for her flaringly bell-shaped wide buttock-cheeks. Like daughter, like mother, he thought. Her aroma was exhilaratingly stimulating to him.

Valerie removed her brassiere while Mark was steering her toward the bed. She got one stocking off while he was placing her on her back, but she still had one on when he was between her wide-parted legs and lowering himself on her smoothly rounded belly. He held himself slightly to one side so he could finger-frig the darker cunt-hole at the end of Valerie's pink gash, but when his finger encountered her flowing juice he removed it and immediately substituted his big prick.

"My, but you're—ready—this morning!" Valerie panted as the knobby head thrust into her moist jewel box. "Ahhhhh, that's—grand, dear!"

A fleeting image of Penny's yieldingly firm young bare behind thrust itself into Mark's consciousness, and then was gone as he concentrated upon the warm, oozing chasm into which he was forcing his lengthy gristle. Valerie whistled like a teakettle as her depths were probed by the husbandly stout cock, and Mark began to stroke in and out of her well-lubricated quim as her hands settled firmly upon his shoulders.

"Like—it?" he grunted between plunges upon the wonderfully pliant warm flesh.

"Love—it!" Valerie returned blithely, throwing her bottom up to meet her husband's spearing thrusts. "Ohhhhh, darling, I—love it!"

"Love—what?" he demanded.

"Being—fucked by—you, dear."

They both fell silent as the two naked bodies matched submersion and engulfment as Mark's prick plunged furiously into Valerie's distended cunt-sheath. His wife's animatedly agitated broad bottom gave new life to Mark's scouring cock. "Ahhhhh!" Valerie exclaimed in-voluntarily. "Ohhhhh! I'm—Mark!" She slowed down her frantic ass-pumping momentarily, then redoubled it as her orgasm overtook her. "Ohhh, ohhh, ohhh! I'm—*coming!*" Her stomach fluttered wildly as her cunt-walls contracted and bedewed the ravaging prick buried in her. "Ohhhhh-h-h-h," she mourned. "I wanted—to make it—last!"

Eyes glazed with unslaked lust, Mark pounded his wife's upturned dripping pussy with belly-whopping effort that resounded in the bedroom. Valerie thrust herself upward again to make the best possible platform for the big prick that was jackrabbiting into her sex-slit. She could feel Mark's hairy balls slapping her anus with increasing speed and force, and she flung her arms tightly around this man who had relieved her so delightfully of the burdens of her widowhood.

She reveled in the sensation as he almost stood on the tip of his prick as his hot jism shot the length of his cock and inundated her already dripping interior. For long seconds he remained rigid in her arms as spurt after spurt of his heavy cream shot into her gaping twat, and then he sank slowly down upon her as if his bones had turned to water.

"That was wonderful, dear," she murmured gratefully as he began to stir upon her. Their perspiring stomachs made a sticky sucking noise as they parted. Mark went into the bathroom and returned with a warm washcloth with which he gently and thoroughly washed every inch of Valerie's sexual parts. "Thank you, darling," she said, stretching languidly on her back and then rolling onto her stomach. "Ahhhhh, God, I feel glorious!"

"Why don't you take a little nap before we go out to the airport to pick up Neal?" Mark proposed.

"I'd love to if I have time," Valerie answered, trying to see the alarm clock.

"I'll call you," Mark promised.

He went into the bathroom again and took another shower. By the time he was dressed, Valerie was snoring slightly. Mark smiled tolerantly at his wife's sprawled, full-fleshed nudity, and drew a sheet up over her. Then he went out into the hall.

Ethel was just passing their bedroom door on her way downstairs. She took one quick look at Mark, another at the clearly-outlined nude figure of her mother under the sheet in the bedroom, and the girl's nose and chin tilted scornfully into the air. She went down the stairs without a word.

Mark smiled to himself as he followed.

The family drove to the airport to pick up Neal, Mark driving with Valerie in the front seat, and Ethel and Penny in the rear. Only the exuberant younger sister contributed much in the way of conversation during the drive. She had started to act standoffish with Mark when first she encountered him downstairs that morning, but he had passed it off lightly. "Hi, kitten," he greeted her casually, and kissed her on the cheek. Penny was both charmed and disarmed.

At the airport Penny was the first to greet Neal. She sprinted a dozen yards to fling herself into his arms and kiss him soundly on the cheek, standing on tiptoe to do it. The tall, sandy-haired, blue-eyed boy patted her shoulder awkwardly.

Mark watched in amusement as Ethel went forward more sedately to offer her own greeting. Both girls wore skin-tight jeans. "Those jeans!" he murmured to Valerie. "How in the world do they ever get into them? Their backsides look as though they'd been poured into them like jello and then hardened."

"I can tell you how," Valerie returned. "They wash them and put them on still damp, so they literally dry right on the flesh."

"Some flesh," Mark said drily. "The in-seams look as though they're drawn right into the crotches. Don't they give themselves some sexual excitement just by walking with the jeans so tight against their little cunts?"

"Would you deny them their simple pleasures?" Valerie asked with a smile.

"By no means," Mark said emphatically. "By no means. I was just curious."

He would have said more, but Penny and Ethel led Neal toward them. Neal made a formal little bow to Valerie,

86

who kissed his cheek, then shook hands with his father. Valerie was reminded that the boy was almost as tall as Mark, although just beginning to flesh out his lean frame. There was just a few weeks' difference in Neal's age and Ethel's.

Neal had only a handbag, having shipped the rest of his things, and when he had stowed that in the trunk of the car, Mark took his expanded family to dinner. He had reasoned earlier that a meal in a public place would be a better ice-breaker than returning home immediately, and so it proved to be. Penny chattered vivaciously, Ethel entered into the conversation with more restraint, and even the shy Neal blossomed under the joint feminine attention devoted to him.

Valerie ate with a good appetite while she watched the boy. Neal had a really brilliant smile when he felt relaxed enough to employ it. His manners were excellent, and when his initial stiffness wore off he bantered nicely with the girls. Valerie had no qualms about the success of the venture.

Twice during the meal Ethel lapsed into silence, and Valerie intercepted smoldering glances the girl directed at Mark. The nature of Ethel's obviously adoring look made Valerie feel faintly uneasy; she felt that this was a new and unwelcome facet in the family situation.

But then Mark, who was sitting beside her, placed a hand casually on Valerie's thigh, and a warm feeling of well-being invaded her, demolishing her previous uncertainty. She rubbed her own thigh lightly against Mark's, and thought how happy she was in having the affection of this strong, virile man.

"You may be unhappy to learn that you start school here tomorrow, Neal," she said lightly. "We've made all the necessary arrangements."

The boy smiled at her, disclosing perfect teeth. This youngster is going to break a thousand feminine hearts, Valerie thought to herself. She looked at Penny, plainly dazzled by her new brother. "I'm sure I won't mind at all," Neal said earnestly. He looked around the table at his new family. "I—I hardly know what to say." He smiled again. "I mean it feels so nice just to be here."

"It's nice having you," Penny chirped gaily.

Ethel said nothing, but her eyes took in Neal's lean figure and unexpectedly wide shoulders with a speculative gleam.

Mark drove the Walker family home with a few private thoughts of his own on the permutations he expected to take place.

Tuesday afternoon Ethel went directly home from school. Mark was at the office, it was Valerie's bridge afternoon, and Penny was playing field hockey for the juniors against the sophomores. That left Neal and Ethel at home, and the older sister intended to capitalize upon it.

She had already decided that finesse was too time-consuming. She was confident that she could lure Neal by a slowly expanding aura of feminine attractiveness, but after the deep-seated feelings stirred in her by Mark, she didn't propose to wait. She didn't know exactly what she was going to do as she hurried home, but she was determined to take every short-cut possible toward seducing Neal. The boyish appeal of the winsome-looking Neal made her saliva flow more freely and her panties damp.

She entered the house and went upstairs at once. Neal's bedroom was down the hall from Ethel's with the jointly used bathroom in between. Penny's bedroom was across the hall. Ethel had heard her mother lay the law down to the younger sister: no more flitting across the hall from bedroom to bathroom in her birthday suit, not with Neal in the house. Mark and Valerie's master bedroom and bath were far enough down the hall so that Penny had usually been enabled to make her sprightly dashes without discovery.

Entering her own bedroom, Ethel at once heard sounds from the adjoining bathroom. She didn't even give herself time to think about it; she walked to the door, knocked once, and entered. "Hi," she said breezily.

Neal looked up, startled. The shower was running and he wore only a loosely-knotted towel around his waist. He had been just ready to step under the steaming water. "Oh, hi," he returned weakly. Ethel's seemingly cool, sophisticated manner intimidated him. "I like—I like to take a shower after school."

"Am I invited?" Ethel asked coyly.

Neal smiled, having no idea that she meant it. "I should be so lucky," he said with more than a hint of wistfulness.

Ethel's eyes glowed as she surveyed Neal's broad shoulders, slim waist, and hairy legs. His skin was clear and fresh-looking with light patches of curly fleece on his chest. Ethel went to him, reached under his towel-loincloth, and took his penis in her hand.

Neal instinctively tried to back away, but Ethel held firm. "What—what are you *doing?"* he stammered, his features flushing.

"Looking at your prick, if you'll stand still," Ethel said coolly. She raised the towel and studied her captive. "Say, that's really a nice one, Neal." The boy's young organ already had his father's length although not its breadth. Ethel squeezed it in her palm, and Neal came up on his toes.

"Take it—easy!" he gasped. "You don't know—what you're doing—to me!"

"Oh, yes, I do," Ethel replied confidently. She removed his loincloth entirely with a sudden grab of her free hand. "There. Let me play with it a minute, Neal."

Her playing resulted in a quick elongation and hardening of Neal's blue-veined long cock. His face turned crimson, and the muscles in his thighs jerked spasmodically. "Ethel!" he got out between clenched teeth. "I'm—you're—I'm—" His voice trembled and he had to stop speaking.

Ethel removed her attention from the vibrant prick jutting forth firmly from Neal's bristly bush while she looked up into his face. "Have you ever fucked a girl, Neal?" she asked curiously. Her hand continued to lightly massage his throbbing cock.

Neal hesitated. He would have liked to boast, to brag, but he sensed that he was already in over his head. "No," he admitted, his lips squirming at Ethel's feathery touch upon his sex organ. "It was dormitory life at school, and—and when we went out it was always in groups. I've—I've hardly been alone with a girl." His lips thinned. "Ethel, please—I'm—I'm going to have an accident!"

Ethel released the stiff-standing penis while she looked Neal in the eye. "Would you like to fuck me?" she asked.

"Would I!" he said fervently.

Ethel at once took charge. "Turn the water off and come into my bedroom," she directed. Neal did as he was told, his flesh quivering in anticipation.

Naked, he confronted Ethel in her bedroom. "What if we get caught?" he asked in a whisper.

"We won't," she assured him. "Nobody is due home for at least an hour, and if we do hear someone, you just run into the bathroom and lock the door and start showering."

"Listen, I'm chicken about this," he said slowly. "I don't want to get sent back to that damn military school."

"You won't," Ethel said. She started to remove her dress. "Relax, Neal. We're going to have fun."

He fell silent as Ethel swiftly peeled out of her slip, bra, and panties. Neal's eyes bulged as they took in her femininity, unadorned except for garter belt and stockings. He groaned aloud as he reached for her and drew her close to him.

Ethel waited quietly while Neal's hands raced over her, stroking her long back and flaring bare buttocks, pulling her belly in against his own while her stomach was jabbed by his fierce erection. "I've got—to see!" Neal said hoarsely, and pushed Ethel backward to the bed.

She went down on her back and offered no resistance as Neal feverishly parted her legs. He ran a finger through her red-bronze curls, and then traced the course of her salmon-pink sex-crevice. She wriggled slightly and sighed. "Mmmmmmm, that feels good, Neal," she said softly.

His face was just inches away from her snug, pouting-lipped pussy. "That's—beautiful," he said quietly. "I've never seen one so close before."

Ethel slithered sideways on the bed to make room for him. "Lie down with me and kiss my titties, Neal," she directed. "You'll like that."

Neal fingered the dewy pink cunt for another few seconds before leaving it reluctantly. He stretched out beside Ethel, started to lower his head toward her firmly-rounded, ruby-nippled white breasts, then paused to look down into her face. "How do you know so much about all this?" he demanded.

"I don't know all that much," Ethel instinctively defended herself from the unspoken charge of promiscuity. "I was hoping we could find out together."

"But you're not a virgin?"

"No. Now no more questions, all right?"

"All right." Neal dropped his mouth upon Ethel's nude breast and lipped at its silky surface. The sensation made him wild; for five minutes he played with mouth and tongue and hands over every inch of Ethel from neck to knees. Again and again he returned to her soft buttocks, kneading and squeezing and caressing and cuddling her velvety nude hind cheeks. His face grew scarlet again, and Ethel became alarmed.

"Neal!" she said warningly. "You're going to shoot! Put it in me first!"

She widened and elevated her long, slender legs, and Neal moved in clumsily between them. He aimed his red-tipped prong at Ethel's deep dimple, but lost his target when he crouched down over her belly. "Where—is it?" he gasped. He shuddered as Ethel's hand slipped between their thighs and recaptured his straining penis.

"Let me do it, Neal," the girl whispered, steering the blunt head to her vaginal orifice. "Ahhhh! Now push, but slowly."

"Ohhhhhh, God, what—a *feeling!*" Neal groaned as he began to thrust into Ethel's already moist channel. She could feel the long cock distending her tight sheath, not painfully as Mark's had, but delightfully. Neal paused for a second, and then his slim hips began to jerk uncontrollably. "Oh, God!" he cried out. "I'm—I can't *stop!*" Ethel cradled him between her clasping knees as his jet-propelled sperm cascaded up into her twitching slit. Neal collapsed upon her, almost sobbing from emotional frustration. "I didn't—even have it—*in* you!" he croaked miserably. "All the way."

Ethel massaged his bare back with both palms. "Rest a minute," she whispered. "Maybe it will come up again."

"I wanted to really *screw* you!" Neal said in despair.

"Shhhh!" Ethel soothed him. "Wait." Her hands stroked the young male body, muscularly hard and terribly exciting to her. She raised her head and blew gently into Neal's ear. He shivered, and a slow stirring took place in his flesh embedded in hers. "There, see?" she comforted him. "Pretty soon it's going to be hard again."

They both almost held their breaths as Neal's prick once more dilated the cunningly clasping sheath. Ethel felt an awesome sense of power that she could provoke this reaction from a male. The semi-resurgent white cock stiffened rapidly, and Ethel cried out as new depths were probed in her slaveringly wet interior. Neal grunted as he shoved at her flesh, and Ethel strained to capture all of the hard gristle within her slippery chute.

Neal began to move upon her experimentally, and a fiery torch ignited in Ethel's cunt. An overpowering feeling of sensual abandon overtook her as she thrust her belly upward. "Fuck me, Neal!" she rasped hoarsely. "Go ahead—and *fuck*—meeeeee!"

Her excitement triggered his own. Neal hammered inexpertly but deeply at the liquefied upturned cunt, his breathing a husky roar. His cock felt like an iron rod as he slashed in an out of the girl's bronze-mossed sex-cranny. He felt stronger than he had ever felt in his life.

Ethel had a quick mental image of her mother on her back with Mark's thick cock plunged into the welcoming generously endowed full-fleshed cunt, and Ethel's excitement increased. Neal buried his prick in her love-trench with increasing speed and force. "Neal!" she cried out. "I'm—ohhh!" Her hips writhed upward, clear of the bed. "Ooooooh! Hard—er! HARDER! Ohhh! I'm—on fire! Oooooh! Neal! OHHHHHHHHHHH-h-h-h-h-h!"

Her bottom had no more than subsided quiveringly upon the bed again when Neal's hips went into the same stutter-step as before. He exploded his slippery lance into Ethel's juicy pussy as hot jets rocketed from the tip of his prick into the girl's already inundated fissure. Ethel patted

93

his shoulders and hugged him to her as his movements subsided to a gentle rocking motion upon her.

She spoke after a moment. "We've got to stop now, Neal."

"I want to do it again," he said, his voice muffled by his mouth's contact with the curve of her neck.

"We've been here long enough," she warned.

He raised his head to look into her face. "When can we do it again, Ethel?"

"Next week this time, if we can't arrange it sooner," she promised.

He raised himself from her reluctantly, and his diminished penis swung damply against his thigh. "How was that one?" he asked hopefully.

"Wonderful," she said softly. "Didn't you hear me?"

He nodded. "I was hoping it was good for you, too."

"Go take your shower," she said in almost a motherly tone. "I've got to clean up, too." He started for the bathroom and Ethel had her first good look at his lean, hard, male buttocks. "You have the littlest behind," she said wonderingly.

"Wait till I get you the next time," he said cockily, and disappeared into the bathroom after waving his cock at her.

Ethel smiled up at the ceiling with mingled tenderness for Neal and tolerance for his suddenly assumed masculinity.

CHAPTER VI

Valerie awakened to bright sunlight streaming in the master bedroom windows, and she rolled over on her back with a contented sigh, raising her hips as she plucked the tangled skein of pink-silk nightgown from her middle and smoothed it downward. She could hear Mark moving around in the bathroom, and she knew she was late, but she was drowsily satisfied to have it so. Conscience stirred her to action after a moment, though, and she flung back the sheet, sat up on the edge of the bed, and felt with her toes for her pompommed mules, a gift from Penny.

She walked to the bathroom with the nightgown swishing between her thighs. She was disappointed to find Mark fully dressed, combing his hair in front of the medicine cabinet mirror. "Good morning, darling," she said, dipping a finger in the water running in the washbasin and quickly scouring her lips and teeth with the finger before holding up her face for his good morning kiss. She had no qualms about bed-warmed feminine odors placed beneath Mark's nose, because she knew he loved them, but she liked to have her mouth and breath sweet for his ardent lips.

"Mmmmmmmmmmmm!" she sighed happily when the long kiss ended. "You're the sexiest thing, husband. I wish I'd wakened earlier and caught you in your shower." Her right hand crept to his belt, then hesitated. "Are you in a hurry, dear? Or may I have a taste?"

"Two minute s," he decreed, and Valerie smiled. She unzipped his trousers and knelt down on the bathmat in front of him as she fumbled his thick-stemmed white cock out of his trousers and shorts. It was damp-feeling from his shower, and Valerie lowered her head and rah her tongue lightly around the blunt head, purplish-red at its tip. Then she wasted no time in swallowing the limp length and began to suck on it strongly.

Mark's hands rested lightly on her blonde head while his wife's hard-working mouth salivated his big penis. In seconds Valerie felt a quick stirring in the husbandly flesh in her mouth, and she sucked harder, ovaling her lips and sliding them back and forth on the increasingly stout rod which was now crowding the back of her throat. A humming sound emanated from her tightly clasped lips, and the vibration transferred to Mark's cock stiffened not only his prick but the muscles in his thighs.

Valerie murmured an unavailing protest as she felt Mark withdrawing his rigid prick from her lips. "Please, dear," she pleaded when the long penis had escaped from her mouth despite her best effort to retain it. "Let me have your come. Please?"

"Wouldn't you rather have it in your monkey?" Mark demanded.

"Oh, yes," Valerie said quickly. "But do you have time?"

"I'll make the goddamn time," he said, reaching down and taking hold of his prick gingerly. "Sonofabitch, Val, for sheer pressure you've got a mouth like a firehose." She giggled, a silvery, rippling sound, and Mark smiled ruefully. "Stand up, Val."

She rose to her feet while he covered the washbasin with bath towels. He doubled her over it sideways, so that her head extended over one edge and her big breasts flopped down into the bowl. One nipple grazed the smooth surface, and Valerie shivered at the quick chill. Mark threw her nightgown up on her back and stared down at her plumped-out, wide-flaring nude white buttocks with tiny tendrils of downy hair showing golden in the sunlight. "By God, woman, you have really got an acre of sweet meat!" he rasped, and spatted his palm sharply on a bare hind cheek.

He did it again, and again, and again. The pistol-like reports of his palm on her naked flesh resounded in the bathroom, and Valerie's broad backside turned pink as it moved languidly under the stimulation. The heat caused by Mark's palm smarting her seat seemed to move immediately into Valerie's moistening pussy, and she tried to lift her bottom higher to meet the palm as her breathing turned husky.

Then the quick, hot spanks stopped and Mark was crowding in behind her. She felt the head of his prick nudging between her buttocks, and the material of his trousers rubbing against the backs of her thighs. Then the delicious big cock ducked down and prodded between her thighs, searching out her slack-mouthed, wet receptacle. The blunt head bumped her groove, and Valerie widened her legs. Mark grunted loudly as the prick-head plunged into her woman-flesh, and Valerie's lips parted in anticipation. Mark grunted again as he surged up into her in a mighty thrust that brought her up on her toes as her entire lower body was lifted upward by the tremendous impetus of the ravaging hard cock in her fiery cunt.

"Ohhhhhhhhhh!" Valerie whispered in muted ecstasy.

He began to fuck her vigorously with quick, hard strokes of his rigid tool, and Valerie wriggled her bottom, writhed, squirmed, danced from one foot to the other, and mewed continuously as her penetrated sex-slit throbbed and pulsed from its disquieting poking. "Mark! Oh, Mark!" she choked. "Ohhh, what a—screwing! Oh, God, I'm *on—fire!* Oooooh! Ohhh!" Her voice pitched itself higher. "Mark! MARRRRRKK! I'm—coming, Mark! Ohhhhhhhhhh, I'm—*coming!"*

Her wriggling behind convulsed itself as her excited sheath grabbed at the fleshy intruder in its depths. Mark picked her up by the hips and ground his iron-hard lance even harder into Valerie's quim as her reaction triggered his own and he shot his load up into her molten interior. He let her go with a long sigh, and Valerie dropped down upon the basin again in a state of semi-collapse.

She raised her head after a moment when Mark pulled out of her with a loud sucking sound. "Ohhhhh, *thank* you, dear," she murmured, turning to face him as he began to tuck his dripping penis into his shorts. "No, wait, darling." She wet a facecloth and quickly washed off his limber tool. "So you won't feel sticky all day." She found a semen-spot on the front of his trousers and dabbed at it lightly with the wet cloth.

Mark stared down at her ivory-fleshed full-figured nudity, as she crouched in front of him at her labors, her nightgown a swirl of pink around her neck and shoulders. He patted a yielding, brimful soft globe that still showed pink from his palm-smarting of it. "I've got to run," he said when Valerie straightened up. He kissed her quickly on the lips.

"Thanks again," she said as he started through the bedroom. "I won't see you until late tonight because of choir practice but that should carry me through." She blew him a kiss as he turned around at the door to grin at her, and then he was gone.

Valerie sighed deeply, considered her tousled hair and flushed features in the mirror, then wandered into the bedroom, nightgown still upraised. She opened her closet door and studied herself in its full-length mirror, her bedraggled, wet-looking pussy-hair failing to conceal her sex-crevice crimsoned from friction.

She turned around and looked over her shoulder at her behind. Both luscious-looking flesh-heavy spheres were still dusty pink from Mark's palm. Valerie's tongue circled her lips. Half a dozen openhanded smacks on her bare seat seemed to make her hotter than just about anything else

Mark did to her. And she remembered her own intense stimulation while watching Mark spank Ethel and Penny. Someday she was going to provoke Mark into an old-fashioned bare-bottomed whaling of her own agitated flesh just to learn the result.

Valerie realized she had forgotten to ask Mark if he would be home for dinner. Sometimes he stayed downtown on choir practice nights. She pivoted away from the mirror and trotted to the bedroom door. She opened it hurriedly, hoping to catch Mark before he left the house. Mark was on the third step from the top, talking to Ethel, who looked up at the sound of the opening door. Conscious of her still-upraised nightgown, Valerie quickly shut the door.

Ethel smiled as Mark turned around too late to see what had happened. "Your bareass wife," the girl said impudently. "Can you tell me what you see in her fat butt?"

Mark reacted instantaneously. His hand dipped under Ethel's skirt and came up between her legs. His palm gripped the girl's thin-pantied crotch and lifted until most of her weight was supported by her palm-supported sex-flesh. Then he squeezed deliberately. "OWWWWWwwwwwww!" Ethel shrilled, her eyes filling with tears as exquisitely painful sensations ravaged her crushed-together pussy-lips.

Mark laughed, and let her go. Ethel sank down upon a step, rubbing at herself. "Stick around tonight and we'll see if your skinny ass is good for anything," he said abruptly, and ran down the stairs and outside to the driveway and his car.

Ethel wobbled down the stairs after a moment and staggered to a living room sofa. Her whole pussy felt as if it were aflame. She leaned back and stretched her legs out gingerly, trying to get all possible weight off her crotch.

And then her lips parted, and her legs stiffened, and her heels slid slowly forward on the carpeting, and her eyes glazed as her perfervidly feverish cunt began throbbing violently in an orgasm that seemed to go on and on and on.

Ethel looked around quickly when it ended.

She was alone, and she went slowly upstairs and changed her panties before she left for school.

In the living room that evening Mark glanced at his watch and then flung the evening paper aside. It was seven-thirty, and Valerie had already been at choir practice for half an hour. Marie left his chair and climbed the stairs, passing the girls' bedrooms en route to Neal's.

He found his son reading a biography of Napoleon, and he smiled. "Thinking of becoming a professional soldier, Neal?" he inquired.

Neal sprang to his feet, putting the book down, in a residue of his military school manners. "No, sir, but I find it kind of fascinating. The campaigns. I don't understand much about the politics."

"I don't believe I ever did," Mark said. "No homework?"

"No, sir." Neal hesitated. "We were a little ahead in classwork of what I find them to be here. But I'm sure it won't stay as easy as it is right now."

Mark nodded. He took his wallet from his hip pocket and removed a five-dollar bill which he handed to his son. "Why don't you take Penny to the movies, then?" he suggested casually. "She'd probably enjoy it."

"Say, that would be great!" Neal enthused. "Thanks, dad."

"It's okay," Mark said, and left the boy's room. He went to the master bedroom and waited there until he- heard Neal and Penny clattering down the stairs with Penny's infectious giggle, so much like Valerie's, floating on the air behind them. Then Mark left the master bedroom and walked to Ethel's room.

She was stretched out on the bed with her eyes on the door. Expecting him, Mark knew. He walked in with a deliberate stride, not bothering to close the door. Tonight he had determined to bring things to a head in this house.

Ethel was eyeing him defiantly, Instead of her usual attempt at sophistication, she was dressed in a little-girl style that Mark found appealing. She had on a short dress with a flared skirt, below-the-knee dark blue socks, and bedroom slippers. Mark unfastened his tie, removed it, and began to unbutton his shirt.

"Wh-what do you think you're doing?" Ethel said as Mark unbelted his trousers, and despite herself there was a quaver in her voice.

"I thought we'd find out if you were good for anything except a quick fuck," he said lightly.

"I can do anything *she* can do!" Ethel flared with a quick glance in the direction of the master bedroom.

"That's what I'm here to find out," Mark declared, tossing aside his underwear. The hard-looking, hirsute male body seemed to dominate the frilly, feminine bedroom. "Strip. We're alone in the house."

Ethel rose to her feet uncertainly. One hand went slowly to the fastening at the neck of her dress, then stopped. "What—what are we going to do?" she faltered. Obviously she found Mark's easy self-assurance disconcerting.

"First you'll suck my prick," he told her.

Ethel stared. "Suppose—suppose I don't want to s-suckit?"

"Look," Mark said in a weary tone, "the reason your mother is so good in bed is because she not only knows what a man likes, she anticipates him and does it before he can ask her. Or tell her, like I'm telling you." His hard male grin impaled Ethel's nervous eyes. "What ever gave you the idea the female called the shots?"

101

"Chivalry," Ethel began. "It—"

"Chivalry is in the dictionary next to shit, shellac, and shinola," Mark interrupted her. "Now get your goddamn clothes off before I get them off for you."

Ethel swallowed convulsively but unhooked her dress. She drew it over her head slowly, then followed suit with her slip. Her white shoulders and thighs glistened in the light as she stood there momentarily in bra, panties, and long socks before her hands went to the clasps at the rear of her brassiere. She shrugged the shoulder straps of the bra down and removed the cups from the wine-colored nipples adorning the darker centers of her perky full breasts.

Still more slowly, she slipped down her panties, revealing once more the bushy, bronze triangle of pubic hair Mark had seen at his office. "All right," he said briskly, walking to the bed and sitting down on it. "Kneel down here between my legs."

Ethel's eyes were upon the bunched male flesh at Mark's groin. She approached him gingerly and knelt down in front of him with her hands on his bare thighs. She started to lower her head, then looked up into his face. "Suppose I get s-sick?" she pleaded. "Why don't you just—just fuck me?"

"You won't get sick," Mark told her. He smiled at her cynically. "You females all love the taste of a prick." His smile widened at Ethel's shrinking expression. "Your mother would just as soon have it that way as in her cunt."

The challenge stirred the girl as Mark had intended it to stir her. Ethel waited no longer, but dropped her mouth down upon Mark's lazy erection and flicked her tongue at it. Emboldened, she licked it lightly, then took it into her mouth with a squinched expression around her eyes. Her mouth worked gently as she tried to accommodate the expanding monster.

"Is that so bad?" Mark demanded.

"No," the girl mumbled with her mouth full of blue-veined cock.

"Then suck it," Mark directed. "Suck it hard."

Ethel compressed her lips and moved her mouth along the shaft, back and forth. Her cheeks hollowed as she caught the knack of it and began to suck with more abandon. In the bureau mirror Mark could see the spread of the girl's solid yet delicate-looking bare behind as she crouched in front of him.

"Harder," he said again. He could feel the quick throb of the head of his cock in the girl's soft mouth as jet-propelled sperm spasms lanced through his rigid penis and into Ethel's throat. Mark locked his hands behind the back of her head as she tried to pull away, and Ethel choked, swallowed desperately, gasped for air, and swallowed again.

The excess of Mark's sticky come ran down from the corners of Ethel's mouth onto her chin from where it dripped in long strings onto her breasts. Mark held her tightly as she still tried to back off from the male gristle lodged between her lips. Ethel made faint mewling noises intended to indicate her unhappiness with the cocksucking act Mark had forced her to engage in.

He let her go finally, and she sank back on her heels, scrubbing at her lips with one hand, her cranberry-nippled breasts glistening with quick-drying jism. "You'll make a good cock-sucker eventually," Mark told her, and watched cynically as the impact of his taunting remark shamed the girl additionally.

He sent her to the bathroom for a damp towel and made her wipe off his greasy prick and balls first before she cleaned her breasts, chin, and mouth. The warm caress of the wet towel rapidly restored his virility, and he took Ethel by the arm and drew her over his bare thighs, face down. She stirred uneasily on his lap, humiliated by the spanking position which exposed her backside, naked to her stocking tops, but also aware of Mark's rejuvenated cock probing at the lower portion of her bare belly.

Mark parted the girlish hind cheeks casually and studied Ethel's pale anus snuggled in the depths of her soft globes. Wisps of reddish hair straggled from the puckered girlish asshole to the pouting, pink-lipped sex-groove. Mark slipped the tip of a finger into Ethel's tight anus and wriggled it about as the girl tried vainly to clench her buttock-cheeks and violated buttonhole to repel the intruder.

"Not—*there!*" she gasped, thighs thrashing.

"Why not there?" Mark asked coolly. "D'you ever have a problem getting big shit-turds out of your asshole? I think you need a little loosening up."

He could feel her shrinking both physically and at the image his words were intended to provoke. Essentially he was killing time, but he was also enjoying himself. He planned to delay Ethel's fucking until he was sure that Valerie would walk in upon them. He was curious to see what Valerie's reaction would be, as well as to witness the mother-daughter confrontation.

He continued to play with Ethel's ass while he probed more deeply into her flinching rectum with his hard-boring finger. He nodded satisfiedly to himself when he noticed the tension going out of Ethel's nude thighs. Fleshy opposition to his finger decreased, and with her sphincter bypassed Mark forced his finger in until his knuckle rested snugly between the girl's perspiring hind cheeks. He could hear Ethel's rapid breathing, and he could see that the nape of her neck had turned bright red.

He withdrew his finger only when the girl stopped fighting the insertion. The finger emerged from the warm-rubbery cave with a loud popping sound. Mark at once hoisted Ethel's bare bottom even higher on his lap, dropped his hand down between her thighs, searched out the entrance to her moist sex grotto, and began to frig her slowly. Little ripples of sexual emotion danced through the girl's flesh, and she sighed deeply. There was no resistance now. Languorous stirrings of nubile girl-flesh surrounding the penetrating finger excited Mark's prick so that it thrummed against Ethel's nude, smooth-curving belly.

He raised her from his lap finally and put her on her back on the bed. He went to her bureau and tilted the mirror so that the bed's occupants could see themselves. He parted Ethel's below-the-knee-blue-socks-clad legs and lowered himself on her belly, rubbing his rigidity the length of the girl's bronze-haired coral-colored furrow while she wriggled with pleasure before locating her cunt-entrance and beginning to stuff it with his hard tool while Ethel's breath whistled.

"Ohh! Ohh! Ohh!" she kept murmuring as the big prick distended her cunt-sheath. Her legs shot up in the air and her thighs trembled. "Ohhhhhhh!" she exclaimed as she came suddenly while Mark still lacked an inch or two of full penetration. Ethel writhed and moaned beneath him while he rested.

He pulled out of her then and got on his back and made the girl sit down on his long cock. When it had glided upward into her freshly lubricated chasm, Mark pulled her upper body down on his chest. "Look," he said, and Ethel turned her head to see her own widespread bare buttocks in the mirror with Mark's thick-shafted prick thrust upward between them. She ducked her head down on Mark's chest in confusion.

He fucked her slowly in the female-superior position until Ethel came again with shuddering little cries and quick-fluttering jerks of her stomach muscles. Ecstatic pleas for more from Ethel's lips were interrupted by the sound Mark had been waiting to hear, the closing of the downstairs door. He immediately put Ethel on her back again, inserted his long cock hurriedly, and began to fuck Valerie's older daughter savagely as the girl responded with passionate abandon.

Valerie glanced around the deserted living room before ascending the stairway. Where was everyone? she wondered. Usually Penny watched television after finishing her homework. She reached the head of the stairs and glanced into the master bedroom. There was no sign of Mark, either. And then a series of faint sounds drifted down the second floor corridor, and the hair at the back of Valerie's neck raised slightly.

For a moment her mind fought against acceptance of the texture and pattern of the sounds, but she found herself hurrying along the hallway before she realized what she was doing. The sounds grew louder, and Valerie was agonizedly aware what she was going to see before she stopped at Ethel's open door and with a knifelike pain in the region of her heart stared at the frenziedly coupled pair on the bed.

Ethel's blue socks were elevated ceilingward as her thighs clasped Mark's body with his big cock pistoning in and out of her upthrust, yearning cunt. "Ohhhhh, Mark!" the girl was calling frantically. "Ohhhhh! Ooooooh! It's so—gooooooood!" The girlish behind pumped itself upward to meet Mark's slashing prick-assaults on the crimson, oozing cunt. "Ohhhh, I'm—coming! Ooooh, I'm commmmmmmm-mmming!" Ethel half-shrieked in sexually delirious abandon as Mark grasped her bottom-cheeks to attain more leverage as he fucked her. Then his shoulders writhed and his back arched and he made a roaring sound deep in his throat as he splashed Ethel's relaxed cunt with a huge load of sperm.

The paralyzed tautness left Valerie's muscles. She darted across the corridor to check Penny's room, then Neal's. A wave of relief enveloped her that both were

106

empty. She didn't know what she would have done if she had had to attempt to explain this—this situation to those two. She marched grimly back to Ethel's bedroom and advanced upon the pair still entwined in passion's after-glow.

Valerie could never remember being so angry.

"What do you think you're *doing?*" she cried, her hands pushing and pulling at Mark until she tumbled him from Ethel's sprawled, nude body. Ethel's half-closed eyes flew open, at first in fright and then in defiance. "You slut!" Valerie continued. She leaned down and slapped Ethel's face heavily. "Flaunting yourself in front of Mark, I'll wager!"

Ethel started to scramble from the bed, and Valerie's palm connected solidly with a nude hind cheek before the girl could escape. The pistol-like report echoed in the bed-room. *"Look* at you!" Valerie went on, her own breath a knife in her throat. Ethel glanced down at her crimson belly and sperm-wet fleece and cunt, then glared at her mother.

"Why should he want an old sow like you?" she said shrilly. Mark stooped and began to pick up his scattered clothing. Neither Valerie or Ethel paid any attention to him. Valerie advanced upon her daughter again until they were almost nose-to-nose, but this time the daughter didn't flinch. When Valerie slapped the girl again, Ethel recovered and slapped back. "You let me alone!" Ethel cried. "If he wants to fuck me, you're not going to stop it!"

Shocked beyond measure, Valerie could only stare. Her cheek burned from the imprint of her daughter's palm. Her whole world felt turned upside-down. "You get in bed and stay there!" she said finally, at a loss for further words. "I'll take care of you later!"

Clothes over his arm, Mark left the bedroom and walked naked to his and Valerie's room. Valerie followed, closing Ethel's bedroom door firmly. She entered the master bedroom and closed its door. Mark was sitting on the bed, still naked. He lifted his shoulders in an expressively negative shrug.

"I know she did it to hurt me," Valerie said numbly. She sank down into an armchair with a hand pressed to her lips, and the tears she had repressed in front of Ethel ran down her cheeks. "I kn-know s-she must have t-teased you till you didn't know what you were d-doing, M-Mark."

He rose from the bed and went to her chair, placed his hands upon her quivering shoulders as Valerie sobbed freely, squeezed lightly, then removed his hands as he went back and sat on the bed again.

Penny and Neal returned from the movie to find all bedroom doors closed except their own. "Gee, everyone sure went to bed early," Penny commented. "Guess it's time for us, too. 'Night, Neal."

"No goodnight kiss?" the tall boy teased.

"You're getting as mushy as the movie," Penny giggled. "And you don't mean it, anyway."

"Yes, I do," Neal averred.

Penny started to hold up her glowing young face, then looked around. "Come into the bedroom," she said. "I don't want anyone to see us. I'd feel—funny."

Neal followed her into her bedroom. Penny stopped in the middle of the floor and looked at him expectantly. He placed an arm around her waist and tipped up her chin with his other hand. He placed his mouth on her soft one in a long, lingering kiss. When her lips relaxed, he thrust his tongue between them, and he could feel the tremor that ran through the girl's body.

Emboldened, he removed the hand from her chin and cupped a round breast. "I'll bet you have beautiful titties, Penny," he whispered. He lowered the arm around her waist until it was draped across her buttocks, then squeezed a plump hind cheek. "And bottom."

"You mustn't, Neal," Penny whispered, but made no move to disturb either hand. She wriggled uneasily at the double stimulation but let Mark fuse his lips upon her again while the two disembodied hands roamed more freely. Finally the girl broke away from the prolonged kiss. "Neal!" she exclaimed, half-excited, half-afraid. The hand formerly upon her backside had moved around front and disappeared under her skirt.

"Please let me!" Neal pleaded, running his fingers up the girl's round thighs and probing at her pantied thigh-juncture. He stroked and fondled and kneaded and caressed the tender girl-flesh until Penny's knees felt weak. "Get on the bed, Penny!" Neal continued in a passionately intense whisper.

"We mustn't, Neal!" Penny murmured, but allowed herself to be led to the bed. "What—what are you going to do?"

"I want to see your pussy," Neal replied, his experience with Ethel giving him confidence. He started to raise Penny's skirt.

She captured his hands, frightened but stimulated. He gave her another kiss, and her soft mouth relaxed as his tongue probed for hers and twined around it. "Close the door, Neal," she whispered when her mouth was freed again.

He walked quietly to the door and closed it. When he returned to Penny, he sat on the bed and stood her between his knees. He lifted up her skirt and wordlessly indicated that she was to hold it up for him. Penny clamped it under her arms as goosebumps crawled on her flesh while Mark slowly drew her clinging pink panties down over her hips and left them in a rolled bunch at the backs of her knees.

109

Neal's eyes stared at the chubby expanse of sleekly nude girlish hind cheeks immediately before them. Penny held her breath as Neal's palm traced her full curves and played with her resilient flesh. Then she felt his warm breath and the quick pressure of his mouth as he kissed each brimful cheek, reminding her of Mark. Did all men like to kiss girls' bare behinds, she wondered? It certainly felt nice.

"Turn around, Penny," Neal said.

She hesitated, feeling shy despite her liking for the tall, sandy-haired boy. His hands on her bare hips faced her about, and Penny closed her eyes when she felt his gaze upon her black-fleeced mound and dimpled slit. His hand was there immediately, tracing her lightly dewed sex-lips, pressing between her thighs to explore more freely. Neal finger-pressured the mostly soft flesh with mounting excitement, his prick straining inside his shorts.

Finally he rose to his feet and began unbuttoning his shirt. "Take your clothes off, Penny," he said quietly. He removed the shirt and unzipped his trousers.

She didn't pretend to misunderstand his intention. "What if I should have a baby, Neal?" she pleaded.

"You won't," he said confidently, and knelt down in front of her to remove her shoes. He stood up and slipped down his shorts, took Penny's hand, and placed his erection in her palm. She examined the blue-veined hard cock interestedly while Neal fumbled at her clothing. Penny assisted with her own unveiling finally, then stood quietly as Neal kissed her nipples and played again with her unclothed wide buttocks.

Neal stepped away from her long enough to strip the bed down to the sheet, then sat Penny on it. For a few moments he kissed and patted all the available girl-flesh until his erection became painful. Then he put the still half-frightened girl on her back and moved in between her parted thighs. He stroked her furry mound delightedly, then

110

introduced the tip of his prick to her sex-opening. "I'm afraid of its hurting," Penny worried.

"Just for a few seconds," he soothed her, working his hips as he gained ground inside her taut passage. "Hold onto my shoulders, Penny."

She did as she was instructed, lips pursed against the stretching sensation taking place down in her private parts. How could that long thing go in her slit? Yet she had seen Mark's, much thicker, romp around in her mother's sex-channel.

"Oww!" she whispered as Neal's blunt-headed instrument lodged tightly inside her. "That's as far as you can—"

Neal slammed his hips forward, and a half-smothered cry escaped the girl. With a ripping, tearing feeling, the long cock scraped the depths of her tender inner surfaces. Her pussy throbbed with pain as Neal rested on her stomach. Then the pain eased, to be replaced by a tingling, smarting sensation.

Neal was too inexpert to give her an orgasm, but he came twice himself. Penny felt an unfulfilled ache, but she knew Neal was enjoying himself tremendously, and she tried to be satisfied with that. Her arms encircled the tall boy whose prick was surging in and out of her delicate cunt, and she tried to anticipate what would give him more pleasure.

It was late when they separated on the bed after a long good night kiss.

Neal turned out all the lights and padded silently to his own room in the darkness.

Penny fingered her aching pussy gently and wondered if there was something the matter with her that she couldn't enjoy it the way her mother did. She fell asleep dreaming of a long, white cock.

CHAPTER VII

When Valerie awoke in the morning, an hour before her regular time, Mark was still sleeping. Valerie's sleep had been troubled and far from sound. She had permitted no discussion at all of the situation she had discovered the previous evening. "We'll sleep on it, Mark," she said firmly. "We're not in a rational enough frame of mind to discuss it without rancor now."

Awake in the early-morning stillness of the house, Valerie wondered briefly if she hadn't dreamed it all. But no; in her mind's eye she could still see Mark's hairy buttocks plunging upon Ethel's nudity as her daughter's enthusiastic hip-response welcomed Mark's thick-stemmed big prick into her cunt-sheath. It was unbelievable, Valerie told herself. How could they have come to this state?

It crossed her mind that in the tumultuously upsetting events of the evening just past she hadn't checked on Penny as she made a ritual of doing before her own retiring nights. Valerie slipped from the bed without waking Mark and threw a lightweight robe on over her nightgown. She opened the master bedroom door quietly and walked down the hallway to Penny's partly opened door. Even before she reached it, Valerie could hear the sound of the bathroom shower running. She wasn't surprised to find Penny's bedroom empty.

She stood in the doorway for an instant, running her eye over the reassuringly familiar sight, then paused. Even from that distance she could see dark blotches on Penny's rumpled bedsheet. Valerie approached the bed with lips compressed. She had trained both girls to wear panties to bed beneath their pajamas, and to go to bed napkined a day before their periods were due. Bedsheets were one thing, but blood-soaked mattresses were another.

Even before she reached the bed, however, Valerie's glance had taken in the other telltale signs. Unbelievingly she reached down a hand and touched the semen-stiff sheet areas mingled with the bloodstains. She straightened up, her heart thudding furiously. Was she losing her mind? Instinctively she started across the hallway toward the bathroom, then changed her mind. She veered toward Neal's almost-closed bedroom door, thrust it open, and entered.

The sandy-haired boy was sprawled loosely in slumber, one arm dangling over the side of the bed. Valerie shook him by the shoulder, hard. Neal's blue eyes flew open and focused upon her fuzzily. "Neal," Valerie said sharply, "what have you done to Penny?" The boy didn't answer, but his guilt was plainly written in his confused expression. "Oh, Neal," Valerie continued in a voice that trembled in spite of her best effort at controlling it, "how *could* you?" She drew an agonized breath. "She's only a *baby!*"

"She—she wanted it," Neal said quietly. "Honestly."

"A quite incredible response," Valerie said grimly. "She's not old enough to know what she wants. Now you listen to me, young man. You march right down the hallway to your father's bedroom and tell him what you've done. Right now. I'll wait here for you."

Neal hesitated, then threw back the covers. He had slept nude, and Valerie had a quick glimpse of his young sex organ still bespattered with her younger daughter's hymenblood. Neal went to his closet and shrugged into a robe.

He turned to Valerie again when he was ready to leave his bedroom. "Honestly, it was like I said. She—"

"Talk to your father," Valerie cut him off.

Her eyes filled with tears of frustrated anger, and she sat down on the edge of Neal's bed.

Neal walked down the hallway to the master bedroom, his thoughts in a whirl. Mark was still asleep when

Neal entered. "Dad," the boy said weakly. He repeated it more loudly when Mark failed to stir. Mark blinked, sat up, and looked at his son inquiringly after a rapid inspection of the other side of the bed revealed Valerie's absence.

Neal drew a deep breath. "Penny and I," he began, and stopped. "Last night," he said, and paused again. "We—"

"You screwed her," Mark said.

Neal nodded miserably. "And Valerie found out somehow. She—she just came into my room looking like a—like a witch."

"Did you force Penny?" Mark asked.

"Oh, no, no, no!" Neal said hurriedly. "She was willing. More than willing once we got started."

Mark pursed his lips thoughtfully. His mind was racing. Surely there was some capital to be made of this development? He summed up and discarded several possible courses of action before nodding his head in satisfaction. He fixed his face into stern lines. "You realize, Neal, that Valerie is capable of taking hasty action while upset over this that could affect our pleasant situation here. I assume you find it pleasant?"

"Oh, yes!" Neal said fervently.

"Then a drastic solution is necessary," Mark continued. "Sometimes it's possible to minimize a situation only by contrasting it with another. We need to give Valerie something else to think about. And that's where you come in. Where is Valerie now?"

"In my bedroom, waiting for me to tell her what you had to say to me about—about Penny."

"Good," Mark said. "Now listen to me closely. Everything is going to depend upon you. I want you to go back to your bedroom, close the door, and fuck Valerie."

"Do—do *what?*" Neal stammered incredulously.

115

"She will resist, of course," Mark went on as though his son hadn't spoken. "But you must not let her resistance prevail. And she will not pursue it to the point of calling attention to the situation. I can assure you of that." He looked at Neal sharply. "Can you do it?"

The sandy-haired boy wet his lips with a nervous flick of his tongue. "I—I don't know," he faltered. "I h-hope so. If you say I should."

"I say you must," Mark corrected him. "So get on with it while she's still in your room."

Neal went back down the corridor with a dry throat and a queasy stomach. He went into his bedroom and closed the door carefully. Valerie was still sitting on the bed, trying to keep herself from going to pieces. "Well?" she demanded in a tight voice. "What did your father have to say?" Neal stood in front of her and removed his robe, and Valerie's eyes widened.

"What do you think you're—"

Her voice broke off in a gasp as Neal suddenly pushed her onto her back. Eyes almost starting from her head, Valerie found herself on her back with the naked Neal pulling and hauling at her lightweight robe and nightgown until he had both well up on her plump white thighs. "Neal!" Valerie blurted in a strangled voice. The boy paid no attention. He flipped her onto her side, and Valerie felt her nightwear ascending further until her handsome glistening nude wide buttocks were disclosed. "Ohhhhh!" she bleated.

Almost reverently Neal's right hand delved among Valerie's ample fleshy treasures while she struggled in vain. She flopped onto her back again and Neal seized the opportunity to thrust her nightwear in front up around her neck. His young prick stood forth stiffly, tremendously aroused by the sight and feel of the womanly attractions sprawled before him. "Neal!" Valerie pleaded, but consciously holding her voice down. "No, no, no, no!"

The boy grasped her ankles and spread her legs apart. For a moment he gazed hungrily upon her silky-golden bush scarcely concealing at all the salmon-pink-lipped trench between Valerie's legs, then slid his hands up her smooth legs to widen her upper-thigh stance and make room for himself. Valerie twisted frantically as her stepson plopped himself down on her nude belly with his red-eyed prick, foreskin drawn tightly back, searching for her cunt. "Stop squirming!" Neal demanded.

Valerie's eyes went to the connecting bathroom door behind which she could still hear the shower running. "Not so loud!" she said in an instinctive half-whisper.

"Then hold still!"

"Please, Neal!" Valerie begged. "Don't—ohhh!" The cry was wrenched from her as the stiff boyish prick first jabbed her soft stomach flesh and then dipped down and probed at her hole. "Neal!!!"

But he had gained entrance and triumphantly surged into her plump pussy-lips despite her discomposed tossing and tumbling. "Ooooooooh!" Valerie exclaimed despairingly as she felt the long white prick distend her sex-channel and slowly inch its way inside to its full length. "Take it out, Neal! P-please!"

But the hard young body pinioned her with its weight while Neal delightedly began to fuck his stepmother, pillowing his head on her large breasts while he began to pump his rigid penis in and out of her clinging cavern. The boy gripped Valerie's yielding white hind cheeks in each hand while he redoubled his efforts upon her.

"Ohhhh, God!" Valerie moaned as quick tremors raced through her flesh. Neal turned his head and kissed her on the neck while his hips pistoned his long cock furiously. "Neal!" she wailed.

117

Her legs, which had been resting slackly on either side of the boy's lean body, rose up independently of any direction from her mind and gripped Neal tightly. The pistoning cock was turning her inhibitions to mush as a bright, glowing coal ignited in her interior. To her shamed amazement she found her broad-bottomed backside thrusting upward vigorously to meet each downstroke of the youthful sex organ fucking her so deliciously.

"Ohhh! Ohhhh! Ohhhh! Ohhhh!" she mewed continuously as the up-tempo fucking went on and on, fanning her sexual fever. Lost to the world, she wriggled her heavy behind animatedly as panted phrases tumbled from her drawn-back lips. "Oooooh, fuck me!" she demanded lewdly. "Fuck me! Fuck meeeeee!"

Unseen by her, two doors opened, the bedroom door opening inward from the hallway, and the connecting door to the bathroom. At the hallway door Mark stood motionless with his face set in stern lines. In the bathroom doorway Penny stood with a towel half-shielding the youthful curves which she had been patting dry, her popeyed stare riveted upon the pair on the bed.

"Ohhhhhhhhhhh!" Valerie whimpered as her orgasm overtook her and her stomach muscles began to flutter and her sheath-walls to contract. "I'm—oooooh!—ooooooh!—coming!" Her legs shot ceilingward as her thighs ground away at Neal. "Ohhhhhhhh, I'm—commmming!" Her glassy eyes rolled upward until the whites showed, and her arms wrapped tightly around Neal's upper body.

"OHHHHHHHHH-h-h!"

Valerie's hot-blooded reaction to her fucking stirred Neal's almost immediate response. The boy groaned huskily as the sperm in his balls boiled over and shot the length of his hardworking penis, inundating his stepmother's juicy cunt. He took half a dozen more expiring pokes at that

118

voluptuously agreeable oozing chalice before slowing to a halt.

For a moment there was silence in the bedroom. Valerie raised her head and stared about dazedly for a second before her slowly clearing vision focused upon her husband. "Ohhh, Mark!" she said in a panic-stricken whisper. She tried to dislodge Neal.

Mark moved to the edge of the bed and gazed down at her, his expression angry. "I really felt we could settle our problem, Val, without you finding it necessary to seduce my son," he said in a voice as brittle as glass.

"I didn't mean—it's not what you think—ohh, Mark, I didn't! I d-didn't!" Valerie moaned. After her first effort at dislodging Neal, she clung to the boy as though his young body could effectively conceal her nudity and embarrassing condition.

Neal broke free of her grip finally and rose shakily to his feet, his face red and his prick lapsed. Valerie tried to roll onto her side, but Mark, in his robe, reached down quickly and held her with a palm in her stomach, and for an instant all eyes in the room were upon the friction-reddened, still-throbbing splayed cunt with its triangle-bearded pubic hair stickily damp from Neal's overflow.

"I'm going to find it difficult to forgive this, Val," Mark continued in the same hard tone. "In fact, I believe I'll teach you a lesson."

He removed his hand from Valerie's round stomach and turned to Penny standing wide-eyed in the bathroom doorway. He walked quickly to the doorway, seized her by the wrist, and pulled her into the bedroom. "P-please!" Penny begged, trying ineffectually to cover herself with the towel. "I haven't any clothes on!"

"Appropriate to the occasion," Mark said with pretended savagery, pushing her onto the bed beside her mother. He snatched the towel from her hands, and Penny flinched as her plump-bodied young curves sprang into full view. "This time we'll prove that what's sauce for the goose is sauce for the gander," he declared. He whipped off his robe, displaying his hirsute nudity.

"No, Mark!" Valerie pleaded, divining his intention.

He paid no attention. His right hand darted to Penny's black-haired pussy and his fingers thrust deeply between the girl's thighs. "Ouch!" she whimpered, still tender from her previous night's defloration. "It h-hurts!"

Again Mark paid no attention. He corkscrewed the hand and wrist between the silky-skinned full thighs until they parted. Penny's dainty-looking, fragile-appearing young cunt appeared with Mark's forefinger stuffed into its centerpiece to the second knuckle. He frigged the girl swiftly while his prick rose in an erection that curved it upward from his lower belly.

"No!" Valerie cried again, and tried to scramble toward the pair.

"Hold her, Neal," Mark said instantly, and the boy looped his arms through his stepmother's and pulled her backward until she was half off the bed in his grasp, with her behind wedged against his groin and his hands clasped over the bowl of her white stomach.

Mark returned his attention to the apprehensive-looking Penny whose attention was fixed upon the purplish-red blunt head of the big prick aimed at her mid-section. "You're not going to—to put it in me?" she asked huskily. "It's—it's way too big."

"Oh, no, it's not," Mark declared. He seized and lifted the girl's legs, tipping her onto her back. Her young face stared up at him anxiously. "You'll be begging for more, like your saintly mother."

He pushed Penny into the center of the bed, steering her by her upraised legs as her chubby bare bottom slid over the sheet. Then he climbed onto the bed on his knees and positioned himself in front of the girl with her round white thighs separated by his hands while his wide-stemmed thick-looking prick was poised before Penny's defenseless, pouting pussy. "Ooooh!" the girl squeaked in acute anxiety as she felt the blunt-headed big cock rub against her sex-crevice.

Tears ran down Valerie's face as she gazed helplessly at her younger daughter's embarrassing exposure. Penny squealed again as the big prick parted her tender pussy-lips, then grunted inelegantly as Mark thrust into her. A third of the broad-based cock slid out of sight into the girl's straining cunt, and Penny's breath whistled fiercely as her sex-sheath struggled to accommodate its oversized visitor.

"It s-stings!" she cried out. "It stings!" But her voice had changed by the second time she said it; a rising excitement was overtaking her pained exclamations. "Ohhhh-h-h!" she sighed throatily as Mark worked more of his bulging penis into the girl's upturned gaping slit. "It's s-so—BIG!!"

Penny's round white thighs rose into the air, as her mother's had, disclosing her girlish yet womanly bare bottom. Mark's big prick punctured Penny's thigh-juncture almost to the hilt while the girl made little murmuring sounds. Her hands came up and fondled her stepfather's shoulders as Mark began to fuck her in earnest.

Valerie gazed wet-eyed upon her husband's savage prick-assault upon Penny's inexperienced young pussy. She shut her eyes momentarily at the sight, then opened them again, hating herself for the mixture of shame and excited confusion with which she was viewing the licentiously bawdy scene. She bit her lips in troubled nervousness as Penny began to respond ardently to the plunging big cock ravaging her sex-cranny, knowing just how her daughter felt.

"Ooooooh!" Penny gasped as her pussy turned wanton and grabbed at the stiff pole distending its depths. "I'm—so—oooh! I'm so—hot!" After each belly-whacking lunge into the girl's tight-clasping jewel box, Mark was withdrawing so far that flashing glimpses of his reddish-purple, glistening prick-head could be seen by the semi-hypnotized viewers. Penny's voice went up the scale as the long prick titillated every millimeter of her sex-chute, sending unimaginably delightful sensations throughout her quaking flesh. "Ohh! Ohhh! Ohhhh! Ohhhhh!" she squealed in time to each slashing descent of Mark's slippery penis.

Mark hunched his shoulders and drove harder. The girl was unbelievably tight in the way her oily sheath clasped the circumference of his cock while at the same time she was sexually furnished in a manner that permitted her to engulf Mark's plunging prick as her mother did. Except for the extra sensation afforded by the girl's comparatively unstretched chute in its tingling grip, Mark would have had difficulty in knowing whether it was mother or daughter in whose delectably exquisite cunt he was buried.

"Ohhhhhhh!" Penny half-shrieked as her plump thighs writhed against Mark's ribcage. Each submersion of the blue-veined white cock in her fleece-surrounded orifice seemed to drive her up a long hill where she felt herself delicately poised atop a high, high place. Her belly and buttocks were damp with perspiration as her excitement increased. "Ohhhh, more, more, more!" she solicited her ravager.

Mark had intended to prolong the fucking of his stepdaughter but felt himself suddenly boiling over. His hip movement ran riot as he shot load after load of hot sperm through his quivering tube into the girl's semi-virgin lubricious depths. This final sensation triggered Penny's response and her cunt-walls throbbed violently as her orgasmic shudders matched Mark's and they expired together as Penny's soft moans filled the room.

Mark freed himself finally from Penny's fervent embrace and pulled out of her still-clinging cunt. Penny's reddened pussy-lips showed starkly beneath her black bush, and there was a round pink spot on her firm young belly. She sprawled limply with an arm over her eyes to hide herself from the eyes in the room as awareness overtook her former sexual excitement.

Valerie broke free suddenly from Neal's relaxed grip and crawled across the bed to her daughter. Her right hand delicately explored Penny's wet slit as though assessing possible damage. "Does it hurt, darling?" she asked softly as Mark and Neal both stared at her unconsciously revealed hip-spread as she crouched beside Penny.

"Not really, m-mother," the girl half-whispered.

Valerie kissed her, and Penny returned the kiss.

"Very touching!" Mark snapped in pretended undiluted anger. "Get off that bed, Penny, and come here!" The girl slithered from the bed obediently and approached him with downcast eyes. Mark pointed at Neal whose previously lapsed erection had been half-aroused by the close contact with Valerie's warm buttocks in the position in which he had been holding her. "Suck him off, Penny. Right now!"

"No!" Valerie exclaimed as Penny shyly approached Neal. "Mark, it's—it's *indecent!"* She tried to run to her daughter, but Mark intercepted her. He grabbed her around the waist and held on despite her struggles. "Penny, don't *d-do* it!" Valerie half-sobbed.

"I've seen you do it, mother, and I don't think I'll really mind," her daughter replied diffidently. Meekly she knelt down in front of the wide-eyed Neal and rested one cheek on his thigh before advancing her mouth to the vicinity of his half-aroused erection. With the tip of her pink tongue the girl licked daintily at the sticky head of the boy's penis, which swelled immediately.

"Take it in your mouth!" Mark ordered.

Valerie started to cry again as Penny's dark head moved closer to Neal's groin and the girl's soft lips tentatively surrounded the boy's upstanding prick-head. Mark slapped Valerie so sharply on a nude buttock that she half-strangled on a choked sob. "Stop sniveling and kneel down and suck me!" he demanded.

He slapped her again when she stared at him unbelievingly, and she yipped in pain. She dropped hurriedly to her knees and reached with her right hand for her husband's diminished penis as from the corner of her eye she could see her daughter's lips and mouth gently laving the upper third of her stepson's white cock. Neal's thighs were tensed and his eyes were half-closed as his hands rested lightly upon Penny's smooth bare shoulders.

Valerie lipped at the thick-stemmed cock on her palm and swallowed it, tasting her daughter's sexual juice upon the greasy surface at the same instant she thought of Penny's tasting her own upon Neal's young prick. The thought excited her, and she sucked busily at the limp cock in her mouth which began at once to stir languidly.

Penny moved her mouth experimentally over as much of Neal's long penis as she could get into her mouth, excited in turn by the soft yet rigid feeling of the youthful cock. The girl swirled her tongue around the cock, sensed Neal's quick reaction when she tongued the cord underneath, and paused while she did it again. The boy's thighs quivered, and Penny drew back on Neal's erection until she could lick the blunt, rubbery head. Then she took the prick into her warm mouth again and began to suck as she had seen her mother do.

Valerie expertly tongued and sucked Mark's increasing erection, able despite her position with her face nearly enclosed by Mark's thighs to observe with one eye the slight wriggling movement of her daughter's round white buttocks as the girl busily tongued her stepbrother. The mingled effluvia of Mark's perspiration and his own and Penny's sexual excesses drifted upward to Valerie's nostrils, and she found it sensually enjoyable at the same time she was mentally repelled.

Neal gave up the ghost on trying to contain himself and began to shoot into Penny's straining mouth. Valerie could tell from the girl's strangled gasps what was taking place. Sperm ran down from the corners of the girl's mouth, then dribbled onto her chin. Her eyes were closed as she swallowed convulsively, trying but failing to contain it all.

A high-pitched cynical laugh froze all movement in the bedroom.

Valerie and Penny, the latter greasy-faced, stared over their shoulders.

Ethel, dressed for school, stood in the bedroom doorway taking in the entire scene, and her high-pitched laugh echoed through the room again. "Feeding time at the zoo!" Valerie's older daughter announced scornfully.

Mark pulled his rampant erection out of Valerie's reach when she turned blindly away from the sight of her daughter's superior-looking scornful smile. Penny, as though in defiance of her sister's pronouncement, turned her face to Neal's subsiding cock again and licked delicately at the sticky beads adorning his prick-slit.

Mark strode across the bedroom purposefully and gripped the older sister by an elbow. "You're just in time, Ethyl," he told the older girl grimly. "It happens you've got something I want right now." He reached for the zipper on her skirt and drew it downward.

"You let me alone!" the surprised Ethel cried out as her skirt collapsed about her ankles. Mark swiftly disposed of her half-slip in the same manner, leaving Ethel's lower

125

body clad in pale blue panties from which garter tapes extended at the lower edges, anchoring her dark stockings.

"Shut up!" Mark said rudely, pulling down the blue panties in one extended yank. Valerie, Penny, and Neal had one quick glimpse of Ethel's thick, red-gold bush before the girl turned frantically, displaying her sleekly rounded, full-fleshed dazzlingly milky hind cheeks. The panties, deposited at knee-level by Mark, slowly dribbled down Ethel's calves to join her half-slip and skirt.

Mark re-gripped Ethel's elbow and towed her to the bed. "Don't you t-touch me!" Ethel yelled frenziedly as Mark plumped two pillows together and forced her over them on her stomach, expanding her buttock-exposure to the eyes in the bedroom. She squeezed her thighs together tightly. "You let me alone, d'you h-hear me?"

"Shut up!" Mark repeated, and dealt the exposed backside a stinging spank. Ethel yelped as her soft flesh quivered and the imprint of Mark's palm appeared starkly on a round cheek, at first a pale impression which rapidly turned pink.

Mark leaned forward and let a mouthful of saliva drip downward between Ethel's clenched hind cheeks. He took his hand at once, forced it between her buttocks, and began to- work the saliva into her anus with his fingertip. Ethel squirmed mightily at the painful indignity, her breath coming in quick gasps.

Mark spat on his palm and rubbed the head and shaft of his enormous rigidity. He then looked at the staring Neal and Penny. "C'mere and give me a little spit, you two!" he ordered. He held the backs of Ethel's thighs immobile with his knees as Neal approached readily, Penny timidly. Mark leaned forward and widened Ethel's hind cheeks with his thumbs, exposing the pale aureole surrounding her dark-brown anus. "Spit me a gob in there," he directed his son. "And you—" He addressed Penny. "Slick up my prick."

Son and stepdaughter combined to make slippery Ethel's tightly puckered rear entrance and Mark's stiff-standing, blunt-headed big prick. They both stepped aside finally, and Mark leaned down and applied the tip of his long cock to Ethel's shrinking buttock-flesh. Deliberately he dragged the rampant pole up and down her buttock crease before lodging the tip against her spit-slippery but-tonhole.

"Don't!" Ethel yelled as she felt the pressure. "You'll—split me! You'll kill meeeeee!"

Still on her knees, Valerie watched in fascination. She still blamed Ethel for the unsavory situation into which they had all drifted, and although she found herself unable to wholly approve of the situation, she couldn't repress a faint glimmer of grim satisfaction at the distress of the daughter whose usually haughty, disdainful attitude she found so trying.

"Aieeeeeeeeeee!" Ethel screamed as the head of Mark's prick disappeared inside her rectum with a sudden jolt. "Ooooooooh, no, please! Please!" She was crying openly, choked sobs that wrenched her whole body. "Ohhhhhhhh, it hurts! It *hurrrrrrrrrts!"*

Mark gathered his forces after the strain of the ini-tial insertion and began to batter his stepdaughter's buttock-crease with short, flurrying jabs of his love-muscle. Quarter-inch by quarter-inch he forced his way inside her, reveling in the warm, buttery feeling as more and more of his long cock disappeared from sight. His movements became slightly more free, and those in the room could see the inward and outward stretching of Ethel's distended anus as her pierced flesh clung to her stepfather's probing pole.

A new note of excited uncertainty appeared in Ethel's voice. "It hurts!" she repeated, but no longer with the same positive conviction as before. Mark had settled down to a steady ass-fucking routine which plunged his

127

cock partway in and out of the pliant asshole, leaving only his prick-head always inserted. "It—ohh!—ooooh!—I'm—ohhh!—" She swallowed a sob followed by a startled gasp. "What's—oooh!—happening to m-me!"

Mark reached beneath the girl where her body was humped over the plumped-up pillows and touched her bronze-fleeced cunt. Ethel gave a convulsive little leap unassociated with the spearing of her rectum. Mark separated her moist cunt-lips and fingered the aroused button of her clitoris, and Ethel almost went into a spasm. "Ohh!" she squealed as Mark's hips continued to piledrive his prick into her rectum, which now had a loose-floating, rubbery-feeling area involved with the plunging cock-head. Ethel humped her round-cheeked ass independently of the momentum supplied by Mark, and her frenzied movements stirred him mightily.

Deliberately he plucked each garter tape in turn from its snugly clinging contact with his stepdaughter's bare behind and snapped them on her flesh, but he doubted that she even felt it. He could feel her quick-shuddering orgasm as he manipulated her sensitive clit-bud, and he removed finger and hand from beneath her and seized her by the waist as he slammed harder and harder into her steaming depths.

His own orgasm overtook him suddenly, and the muscles in his thighs stood out like ropes as he braced himself and shot a succession of jet-propelled sperm-loads inside his stepdaughter's rectum. The tip of his prick tickled mightily as it wallowed in her drenched interior. After a moment he withdrew slowly, and the blood-red head of his shrinking cock emerged with a loud popping sound. Ethel lay prostrate on the pillows, gasping, a slow stream of sperm emerging from her crimsoned anus and trickling down her bare thighs.

Valerie, on her knees, stared with mingled emotions.

128

Penny, greasy-faced, and with Neal's arm around her bare waist, stood with Neal's dwindled cock in her right hand as she watched her sister's painful efforts to roll off the pillows.

Mark, briskly businesslike, pointed a finger at each in turn.

"You," he addressed his son. "School. Right now."

He aimed the finger at Penny. "Back into the shower, and then school. Scoot."

The finger switched to Ethel who was delicately exploring her anus with a shrinking finger. "You. Shower and school, after Penny."

The finger poised upon the kneeling Valerie. "You. Into our bedroom."

Without waiting to hear a word in exchange, he strode from the bedroom.

CHAPTER VIII

Mark had left for the office by the time Valerie could pull herself together sufficiently to attempt to face him. After leaving Neal's bedroom, she had gone to the spare bedroom and hid—almost literally hid, she had to admit to herself—until the children had left for school. She felt almost in a state of shock. In retrospect, the events of the morning seemed incredible.

She avoided Ethel, Penny, and Neal upon their return from school in the afternoon. How could she face them? She *had* to talk to Mark first, to try to find out what had happened to them. She had been so supremely happy in her new marriage, so appreciative of all the wonderful sexual games she and Mark played together after she had been without them for so long. Her stomach felt cold at the forlorn prospect of giving up all that, but how could she possibly condone the type of license she had witnessed that morning?

Not only witnessed, but participated in, a corner of her brain reminded her.

She cringed at the thought. What must the girls think of her? What must Neal think of her? She could hardly conceive now her own abandoned role. How in God's name had it all come about? The whole situation was simply unbelievable. Utterly, totally unbelievable.

She had to nerve herself to go downstairs and prepare dinner. Fortunately the children avoided the kitchen as she had avoided them previously. She knew she couldn't say a word to them, couldn't even look them in the eye. She clung to the thought of Mark's return from the office as her only salvation. Although what salvation could there be from this monstrous situation into which the family had somehow drifted?

When she heard the sound of his car in the driveway, it felt as though the weight of the world dropped from her shoulders. Mark would make it all right, she thought desperately. Ever since her remarriage she had been depending upon Mark to make it all right, and he had never failed her. The past few months had been the happiest, the most exciting in her life.

Mark walked into the kitchen breezily, rolled evening newspaper in his hand, smiling widely. Valerie had been so afraid of a continuation of his black mood of the morning that at sight of his smile an icy lump seemed to dissolve in her stomach and her legs started to tremble in relief. She ran into his arms almost blindly, flattening herself against his broad chest. "Oh, Mark!" she moaned piteously. "What are we going to do?"

To her great relief he didn't pretend to misunderstand her. His expression turned momentarily grave. "I've been giving that a good deal of thought today," he said smoothly, "and I believe I've come up with the answer. I'll have a little announcement to make at the dinner table, and then we'll take it from there."

"Oh, Mark, I knew I could d-depend on you!" Valerie sobbed. "This has been the longest day of my life, waiting for you to come home!"

He reached around her and whacked her across the seat with his rolled newspaper, then placed a palm on her pliant buttock flesh through her housedress and slip and jiggled it lightly. "We'll work it out," he said in a positive tone. Valerie's low spirits lifted at the welcome attention to her body from this virile man with whom she was so deeply in love. "Get dinner on the table as soon as it's ready, Val, and we'll proceed to take care of things."

He went upstairs to wash up, and Valerie hurried dinner along via every shortcut she could dredge up from her years in the family kitchen. When she went to the foot of the stairs and called "Dinner!" she felt almost normal again.

The childrens' attitudes as they came to the table gave a quick reminder that the situation wasn't normal, though. No one looked directly at anyone else. Valerie was relieved to hear Mark speak up as soon as Neal had helped Ethel and Penny to be seated and Mark had done the same for her. "Does anyone have an engagement for this evening?" he asked pleasantly.

There was no reply. Neal, Ethel, and Penny stared down at their plates. Valerie sat tensely.

"Then there will be a family meeting in our bedroom at eight o'clock," Mark continued. "I'll expect everyone to be present. Nightwear will be the clothing order of the day. Any questions?"

There were none.

"Eight o'clock," Mark repeated, and helped himself to Valerie's porkchop casserole.

The atmosphere relaxed slightly, but there still wasn't much conversation. Penny and Neal exchanged a few asides, and once Valerie caught Ethel smiling at Mark, but for the most part the family concentrated on food. Mark sat in the living room afterward with brandy and a cigar while Valerie made a pretense of scanning the paper. Neal had disappeared upstairs, and the girls were doing up the dishes.

At fifteen minutes before eight Mark drained off the last of his brandy, looked at Valerie, and rose to his feet. Valerie followed suit and trailed him up the stairs. "What's going to happen?" Valerie asked, unable to restrain her curiosity any longer. "What are you going to do?"

Mark shrugged as he unbuttoned his shirt.

"I'm just going to play it by ear, Val, and hope we're enough of a family to withstand the strains occasioned by this morning's activities." He removed his shirt. "And some of the events leading up to this morning," he added.

133

Valerie didn't consider it a very helpful answer, but she began to undress in a corner of the bedroom. Mark was in the bathroom when Valerie was able to consider her free-flowing curves in the boudoir mirror before she swirled her nightgown over her head and enveloped their luscious amplitudes. She slipped into a robe and sat down nervously on the bed.

Mark came out in pajamas and robe and joined her, and they waited. Penny was the first to arrive, looking subdued. Neal followed shortly, and Ethel was right behind him. Penny seated herself beside Valerie while Neal and Ethel found chairs. Mark wasted no time in speaking up.

"I'm assuming that this is a close-knit family group to whom I can speak freely," he began. No one said anything. "A family group which keeps family matters within the family. In other words, no loose talk outside the house."

He looked from individual to individual in the group. "This morning there were events, happenings if you will, outside the tenets of usual household regimens, yet—" He paused for effect. "No one was hurt. Despite various misunderstandings which led to unusual situations, a certain amount of pleasure was given and taken." He paused again. "Within the family. The more I thought about it today at the office, the more I felt this might be the redeeming feature, this family togetherness."

Valerie was listening closely, trying to divine Mark's purpose. She couldn't seem to fathom what he was driving at.

"So I propose an experiment," Mark resumed. "To take place here tonight in this room, and depending upon its success or failure, perhaps never to take place again. An experience in communal living, for one night, let's say. And we must all agree in advance to abide by group decisions, or leave the group."

Penny looked puzzled, Ethel interested. Neal stared down at his hands in his lap. Valerie tried to read Mark's suave good looks.

"Speaking frankly," Mark went on, "I found the morning's activities stimulating." He smiled. "I'm aware there is a moralistic element in the community and the world which would condemn them. But in retrospect, where was the harm? But you undoubtedly have your own reactions to that question, and depending upon them, you will respond in your own way to my proposal, which is as follows."

Neal looked up from his hand-staring. Ethel was smiling as though at a surmise confirmed, Penny still looked puzzled, and Valerie felt an apprehension she couldn't quite understand.

"I propose we extend the license of this morning to this evening," Mark said. His tone was casual. "To determine if we are truly a close-knit, loving family group. Therefore I recommend that each of us in turn, perhaps in age order, ask to see something or do something in accordance with his or her own desires. Anyone desiring to refrain, of course, is free to leave the group right now."

Valerie swallowed hard. Penny, Ethel, and Neal sat motionless. Valerie tried to tell herself that she should get up and leave immediately. How could she condone this brazen proposal? But how could she walk out of her own bedroom and leave the rest—who obviously had no intention of leaving—to who knew what activity, encouraged by a husband she could no longer understand?

"Since we're in agreement, then," Mark said easily, "let's begin. Penny, as the youngest, what would you like to see or do?"

Penny didn't hesitate. "I'd like to see Ethel's bottomhole to find out if it looks any different after having your big thing in it this morning," she said promptly.

135

"Ethel?" Mark said on a note of inquiry.

Ethel rose from her chair. She nudged a hassock nearer the center of the room, then knelt down in front of it. She pulled her bathrobe up over her shoulders, lowered her pajama trousers, and crouched over the hassock with her sleek-looking bare behind pointed at the group. "I can't see, Ethel," Penny said at once. "Spread your cheeks."

Ethel reached behind herself and parted her soft, plump globes with a hand on each. Her deep crevice flared into view, the white flesh darkened slightly by a thin tracing of red-gold hair in the cleft. The girl's anus appeared centered in her nubile flesh, brownish-pink and puckered-looking.

"Well, Penny?" Mark said.

"It looks the same," Penny said doubtfully. "Although I don't see how it could be, really, after—" She didn't finish. "Is it sore, Ethel?" she asked her sister.

"Tender," Ethel replied in a muffled voice. "That's all."

"Like our bottoms after a spanking?" Penny persisted.

"Very much the same," Ethel agreed.

"Thank you, Ethel," Mark said smoothly. "Now it's your turn, Neal. What would you like to see or do?"

Neal hesitated, glanced quickly at Valerie, and then away. It was plain he was trying to make his voice sound determined when he spoke. "I want Penny to take down her pajama bottoms and then get down and suck Ethel's pussy," he said.

Ethel paused in the act of pulling up her pajama bottoms. She let them fall to her ankles while a slow tide of color invaded Penny's young face. The younger sister rose to her feet, however, and disposed of her own pajama trousers, leaving herself nude from the waist down, her wide-flaring bare seat with its vestigial traces of puppy-fat looking almost polished in the light.

"Get on the bed, Ethel," Mark said briskly, making room.

Ethel climbed on the bed, rolled onto her back, and parted her legs. Valerie shivered as the girl's red-bronze pubic hair and salmon-pink sex-incision appeared. This was—why, this was an unblushing debauchment of innocence almost impossible to comprehend! Yet what could she say without totally alienating the others, whose eagerness was now starkly apparent?

Penny moved onto the bed with her sister, and at once crouched down over her, then prostrated herself on her stomach in front of Ethel, who raised her legs, elevating her fragile-looking cunt and placing it within reach of Penny's mouth. Penny darted a tongue at the target, and Ethel's legs quivered. Penny gave the pouting-lipped porch a half dozen licks, then inched forward and boldly plunged her mouth down upon Ethel's sex.

Neal's, Mark's, and Valerie's eyes were focused upon Penny's soft buttock-flesh trembling slightly from her exertions as she took her sister's whole sexual orifice in her mouth and worried it. Ethel's face slowly turned crimson as she stared up at the ceiling and her sister's soft mouth nibbled at Ethel's moist pussy-lips. "Ohhhhhhhh!" Ethel sighed deeply.

"Don't forget her clit, Penny," Mark advised.

Penny immediately worked her way up her sister's sex-groove, forcing the lips apart with her tongue, until she could attack the little pink bud. "Ooooooh!" Ethel exclaimed at once as her legs jerked involuntarily, almost dislodging Penny from her face-down position. The younger girl pressed her face more tightly to her sister's crotch and tongued the target fiercely.

Ethel sighed and moaned and wriggled as her clitoris was stimulated by Penny's hot young mouth. When Mark saw that the younger sister wasn't expert enough to bring Ethel to an orgasm, he reached over and slightly slapped a sleekly upraised globe of Penny's. "That's enough for now," Mark decreed.

The sisters separated, Ethel with a highly stimulated glow upon her features, and Mark waited for her to recover some semblance of composure before addressing her. "Ethel? What do you want to see or do?"

The older sister spoke so quickly it was obvious she had been thinking about it. "I want to see Neal fuck mother with mother on top," she answered, and smiled maliciously at her mother.

Valerie turned scarlet. Neal was looking at her with an eagerness that in any other circumstances she would have found heartwarming. "Val?" Mark prompted her. His expression was bland, as though the request was the most natural thing in the world.

For a count of ten Valerie sat motionless. A thousand thoughts flashed through her mind, but one predominated. Her sexual happiness with Mark—could she jeopardize it by refusing to participate? She knew it was a selfish point of view, but after her years of deprivation it was so terribly important to her.

She was never aware of making a conscious decision. She found herself on her feet removing her robe, and her nightgown quickly followed it. She went to Neal and took him by the hand, and the boy's eyes glistened with excitement as he rose to his feet and shed robe and pajamas. He took Valerie by the arm and led her to the bed.

"Tickle her up a bit to get her wet, Neal," Mark instructed his son.

Neal had already been stroking his stepmother's soft amplitudes; he dipped a hand between her thighs and began fingering her tumid, swollen sex. Valerie's large but shapely thighs parted to admit the hand, and Neal reveled in stroking and fingering her well-seated cunt. The boy was half out of his mind with pleasurable sensation.

Valerie could feel herself getting moist, and Neal could feel it, too. He slid onto the bed on his back with his hard young prick stiffly erect and beckoned to Valerie. Again she allowed herself no time to think. She straddled the lean young body and lowered herself carefully upon the stiff-standing white cock. It bumped her buttocks and then her legs before she reached under herself to grasp and steer it.

Neal gasped as she deftly aimed his ruby-red prickhead up into her slot and eased herself down upon it. She joggled her hips to settle herself firmly, and when she felt her pubic hairs entwining with her stepson's, she leaned forward gradually along the length of his young belly and began to glide up and down slowly on his rigid pole.

Neal wrapped his arms tightly around Valerie's smooth back and buried his face in the arm juncture between her neck and shoulder. Occasionally one hand would creep downward and play with a handsome bare buttock as Valerie's large bottom agitated itself in a delicious slow-fucking mazurka as Neal's cock filled and refilled her sex-bower.

The boy's excitement gradually inflamed Valerie. Ethel, Penny, and Mark watched with varying degrees of excitement of their own as Neal's sturdy penis appeared and disappeared as Valerie raised herself high enough to lose all but the head and then plunged downward to engulf its entirety in her moist-walled sanctuary. She was almost lost to everything except a haze of sexual pleasure from the young prick piercing the depths of her cloister.

"I don't need to wait for this to finish to know what I want to see or do," Mark said to the girls. "I can do it right now, and I will."

He went to Valerie's boudoir and picked up a jar of cold cream. He unscrewed the top and set it aside before returning to the bed where he took a gob on his fingers and applied it liberally between Valerie's nude hind cheeks which were still rising and falling in carnal gratification. Valerie flinched at the cold impact upon her bare flesh, but refused to allow herself to be distracted from her enormous enjoyment.

Mark worked the cold cream into his wife's buttock-crevice and especially into her anus. Valerie writhed languidly at the additional stimulation provided by the husbandly finger inserted insider her bottomhole to complement the hard rod probing its neighboring entrance. She was close to an orgasm and trying to fight it off in order to prolong the deliriously cosy luxurious contentment in which she was wallowing.

Mark winked at the staring Penny and Ethel. "All aboard what's goin' aboard," he said lightly, and knelt on the bed beside Neal and Valerie. He paused to cold cream the length of his own massive erection, then glanced at his son and his wife. "Hold her, Neal," he said, and moved in behind Valerie's distended, plumped-out bottom-cheeks.

Valerie raised her head as Mark's cold-creamed big prick probed between her roomy, wide-spanned ivory globes. Her eyes which had been half-closed in blissfully lovely self-indulgence flew wide open as her husband's prick-head jabbed at her tight-puckered anus. "Mark?" she said questioningly. "What are you—ohhhh!"

Mark had seized her by the hips and applied the tip of his cock squarely to his wife's rectum-entrance, then pushed. "Mark!" Valerie wailed as she felt herself painfully impaled, but her husband shoved harder.

Valerie struggled desperately to remove her helpless asshole from its tormenting penetrator, but Neal's cock in her cunt and arms around her shoulders prevented meaningful movement. "Owwwww!" Valerie cried out as Mark's purplish-red blunt head disappeared within her buttocks, pulled apart by Mark's hard hands. Fiery pain lanced her anus-aperture as Mark forced more and more of his long cock inside. Tears stung Valerie's eyelids and rolled down her pale cheeks. "No, Mark, p-please!" she begged hoarsely. "Ohh, God, you're *s-splitting* meee! Mark! Owwww! Ooooooh! Mark! Ohhhhh-h-h!"

Her palms flailed the bed frantically on either side of Neal's head as she felt her rectum agonizingly violated by the hot poker inserted into it. Her ragged breathing rasped in her throat and she gasped with relief when Mark stopped grinding his prick inside her tiny buttonhole and rested on her back.

Dimly she heard Mark's voice. "How's that for a fore-and-aft job?" he was saying to the girls. "Quite a sandwich, hmm?"

Neal stirred beneath Valerie, and she felt a quickened renewal of sensation in her prick-filled cunt. The sharp pain in her rear subsided to a hot glow, and tingling, titillating ripples of sensation fanned outward from her doubly pierced orifices. Neal jogged his gristle upward into Valerie's slippery sheath, and her breath whistled sharply.

She tensed when Mark began to move on her again, but she found at once it didn't hurt as it had before. It took her a second to realize that Mark was fucking her asshole in time to Neal's fucking of her pussy from beneath her. The double sensation, the one wholly pleasurable and the other half-painful, spread and permeated every ounce of flesh in her lissome body.

"Ohhhhh!" Valerie murmured as the double-fucking continued. She could feel the two pricks almost rubbing together inside her, separated by but a thin strip of her own flesh. Her voice rose. "Ohhh, Mark! Neal! Ohhhh, it's—oooooh, it's lovely! It's—*lovely!*" Her own movements became uninhibited as the previous pain disappeared in a wave of prolonged delightfully sweet easement. A prick was shooting hot sperm into her, and she couldn't even tell which one. Her own climax was building apace. "I feel—like I was—standing tiptoe—on the head—of a pin!" she got out breathlessly. "Ooooooh, there—it is! I'm—" Her breath husked in her throat, "commmmmming!"

Belly, buttock, and cunt muscles expanded and contracted rapidly in a fluttering symphony, and Valerie sprawled limply between the two male bodies, drained of all emotion except a restful well-being. She was hardly aware that Mark was pulling his prick out of her until she heard the loud popping noise as her rear entrance snapped to behind the departed prick. She felt a renewed glow in her asshole at the abrupt dislocation, but not nearly enough to disturb her grateful happiness.

Mark's cock trickled driblets of jism over Valerie's bare behind, and she became aware that Neal's youthful penis still reposed, rampant as ever, in her pussy. She raised herself on her elbows and placed both palms on either side of the boy's face. "Would you like me to turn over so you can finish off?" she whispered.

He nodded eagerly, and Valerie raised herself gingerly from the stiff young prick, stretched muscles in her rear pulling at her. She rolled onto her back, wincing at the body-weight placed on her tender anus, but immediately raising her legs to furnish a solid platform for young Neal as the boy shuffled forward on his knees and applied his oily-looking reddened blunt rubbery head to Valerie's swimming cunt-hole.

Valerie relaxed in refreshed felicitous ease with her hands patting Neal's hard shoulders as the boy's hips pistoned her channel furiously. Neal plainly was half-delirious with delight as he fucked the big, womanly body which accommodated him so affectionately. Valerie stroked his back gently as the boy worked himself up to a pitch and fired load after load of jetting spend into her already juicy crypt.

"That was beautiful, Neal," Valerie heard herself saying without having any intention of saying it as the boy rolled away from her with a depleted but satisfied sigh. Valerie lowered her legs and half sat up, wincing against as her shifting body-weight again reminded her of her newly pierced rectal orifice.

Ethel was on her knees between Mark's parted legs as he sat on the edge of the bed, busily tonguing and sucking his drooping, reddened cock back to life. Not to be outdone, Penny approached Neal and tugged his legs over the side of the bed, then knelt in front of him and took into her mouth the limp prick so recently immersed in her mother's curly blond-tufted lair. There was silence in the bedroom for a moment except for the soft slurping sounds furnished by the girls' hardworking mouths.

Ethel leaned back from Mark's half-restored erection and looked up at him. "It tastes different this time," she told him.

"It should," he grinned at her. "That's your mother's shit you're getting." Ethel started to back away, but Mark gripped her head and pulled her back onto his prick. "Go on, get with it. It's good fertilizer. It'll make you grow." Ethel's tongue reluctantly resumed its cleansing of the big cock.

Penny's eyes were half-closed in sumptuous satisfaction as she zestfully sucked her stepbrother's greasy penis, which under her devoted ministrations was rapidly nearing refulfillment as it crowded her mouth. The girl's sweetly chubby nude hind cheeks swayed gracefully beneath the slender stalk of her waist as she labored.

"We've forgotten our manners," Mark said suddenly.

Penny and Ethel stopped cocksucking to look at him inquiringly as Neal did likewise.

"We didn't ask Valerie what she wanted to see or do," Mark continued.

All eyes turned to Valerie on the bed. Penny glanced at the others to be sure they weren't paying attention to her, then looked at her mother and first tapped herself on the chest, then pointed to Neal.-The girl's expression was illuminated by a smile that was so mischievous-looking that in younger days Valerie had always referred to it as Penny's I'11-take-a-chance-on-a-spanking smile.

Valerie hesitated under the combined gaze of the others. She sensed that everything else had been prelude, that if she spoke now in the same vein as the previous activities indicated, she was past the point of no return and irrevocably committed to a course of permissiveness that still seemed incredible to her.

Penny impatiently tapped herself on the chest again with a pleading look on her eager young face. Valerie took a deep breath and turned her back on years of instilled rigid morality. "I want to see Neal fuck Penny," she said steadily.

Penny squealed with delight, bounced up from her knees in front of Neal, and plunged at the bed, rolling over on her back in complete puppylike abandon. "Give me a good one, Neal," she admonished him seriously.

Neal joined her at once, nothing loath, as Penny made room for him between her chubby thighs, widened to disclose her pink young cunt in its silky-mossed nest of black hair. The young bodies blended together as Neal's long tool slipped between Penny's pussy-lips and moved slowly upward into her sex-aerie. Penny sighed luxuriantly as she felt the penetration. "Mmmm, that's good!" she mur-

144

mured as her small hand reached out and sought her mother's, on the bed nearby.

"You do me now," Ethel said imperiously to Mark.

"I'll get around to you later, puss," Mark told her.

He swiveled himself back into the center of the bed and knelt beside Valerie. "How about a fuck, old lady?" he said to her with that mixture of bravura and virility which always turned Valerie's bones to water.

"I don't mind if I do," Valerie answered with attempted lightness, but she reached for Mark's hand with her free one—the other was still tightly gripped by Penny—and squeezed it fiercely. This is what it's all about, she told herself quietly. Mark and me, together; in bed, if possible, but together.

He put her on her back as gently as if she were something truly fragile, as though he wasn't the same man who had brutally ravaged her asshole. That was the wonder of the man, Valerie marveled; his mercurial temperament made him a hundred men in one, and all—well, almost all—her particular delight.

Mark moved the hard-fucking Neal and the hard-sighing Penny slightly to one side to make room for Valerie and himself on the bed. Neither of the youngsters noticed the dislocation. Then Mark introduced the head of his big prick to Valerie's fully displayed cunt-hole as she awaited the familiarly passionate provocative distention. "You've got a wet deck tonight, old lady," he said jocularly just before he leaned down into her.

Mark fell silent then. Valerie dreamily twined her fingers in his hair as the wide-stemmed long cock pressured her inner flesh into parting acceptance. He began to ride her slowly, power-diving into her depths which seemed nigh to overflowing with lovely cock, and Valerie's breathing quickened.

Beside them on the bed there was a quick flurry as Neal's hip-plunging orgasm triggered Penny's risibility and the girl's legs climbed as her contracting cunt-sheath bedewed liberally Neal's shaft. Boy and girl lay in each other's arms, panting, reveling in the feel of each other's flesh.

Mark never even turned his head. He savored mightily the glove-tight feeling of his wife's clasping cunt around his prick, and he deliberately held himself down to a moderate pace as he stuffed and re-stuffed every nook and cranny of her prick-hermitage with his fully aroused instrument.

Valerie basked in the deliciously sensual hedonistic abandon with which she accepted the fucking. Nothing else in the world mattered except the wonderfully agreeable, snugly luxurious sensation of Mark's hefty penis in her squirming, palpitating vault. Her besieged flesh felt ablaze from rapturous vibration.

From a corner of her eye she saw Neal and Penny separate, the girl with a pleasantly bemused expression on her face. Ethel at once moved in officiously beside Neal in her usual take-charge manner. She leaned down from a kneeling position to lick at his dwindled penis, and Neal reached up between her thrust-back hind cheeks to insert a finger between them and play with the girl's pussy.

Ethel looked back in surprise at the unexpected fingering, but quickly took advantage of it. She lifted one leg across Neal's body and backed up until her bronze-haired, pink-lipped twat was just above the boy's face. Ethel then simultaneously lowered her cunt upon Neal's mouth and her own lips upon his softened cock, and both began to employ their tongues in vigorous harmony.

Mark fucked his wife with slow, sure strokes that seemed to the panting Valerie to penetrate her more deeply than ever before. At each descent of the pouncing big prick into her sanctum santorum, Valerie thrust upward with all

146

her strength until the velvety surfaces of her rotund naked buttocks swung clear of the bed momentarily before being forced down again in the most delightful manner by the fleshy linchpin connecting husband and wife.

A tremor rippled Valerie's nude body, and was immediately followed by another. "Oh, Mark!" she gasped, squeezing his lean middle between her thighs. "Mark! Oooooh, I'm boiling—over! Ohhhh-h, what *f—feeling!"* She was silent momentarily as she tried desperately to position herself in a way that would permit her to take into her feverishly throbbing cunt even more of the wonderful monster dilating her inflamed sex-fissure. "Oooooooooh!" she moaned in sensuous delight, all demurely ladylike coyness and docile self-controlled femininity vanished in the depths of her passion. "Fuck me, Mark! F-fuck me! Ohhhh, lovely, lovely, lovely!" Her hips flurried madly as her orgasm overtook her, and she sank backward, nearly undone from the excess of her emotion, her arms still clasping Mark tightly as he continued to plow her garden relentlessly.

Beside them Ethel and Neal had swapped positions. Ethel was underneath and Neal on top with his Ethel-aroused penis buried in the girl's sex-trench which quiveringly received each ardent submersion of the boy's fleshy pole. Ethel's long legs were locked over Neal's back as she murmured faint-sounding, almost inaudible endearments to the prick provoking her extremely pyrotechnic pleasure.

Mark's leisurely pace in fucking Valerie accelerated suddenly. She recognized the signs, and wasn't surprised at all to feel his big hands slipping beneath her springy bare behind to grip each cheek tightly as he drew her closer to him while the jackhammer pounding her willing cunt went out of control. "Aaagggrrrhhhhh!" Mark bellowed in her ear as he deluged her interior with his thick cream. Valerie lay back contentedly as the final prick-throbs died out in her overflowing cunt.

147

A rasping sound from Neal's straining throat signaled his climax as Ethel's straining slender legs climbed ceilingward. The boy's shuddering-ly expelled quick bursts of sperm mingled in the girl's molten quiff with her down-pouring of love-juice triggered by her fleshy visitor.

Ethel's legs lowered and splayed widely as Mark raised himself from Valerie's plump, perspiration-filmed, smooth belly. There was silence in the bedroom as Mark swung his legs over the edge of the bed and sat up. Neal rose from Ethel, and he and Mark looked at the flushed, rosy-lipped, slack-looking cunts of mother and daughter.

Penny was standing beside the bed, also watching. Still wearing only her pajama top, she went to Mark and bent down and kissed his cheek. "What are we going to do next?" she asked so wistfully that Mark laughed.

He turned the girl around, picked her up by the waist and lifted her so that her chubby bare seat was at eye level, then leaned forward to kiss each silky bell-shaped hind cheek lingeringly. "I don't know what we're going to do, kitten, but we'll think of something," he assured her, slapping her bottom as he released her. "Now give your mother a kiss."

Valerie opened her arms as her younger daughter flung herself upon the bed and pressed warm kisses upon her lips, the soft young body blending with Valerie's.

She, too, didn't know what was coming next, but she was prepared now to block out thoughts of the future in favor of sensations of the present.

NINETY DAYS LATER

Valerie Walker bid four hearts and listened for her partner's response after the intervening pass. She was at her regular mid-week afternoon ladies' bridge session, and at the four tables around hers the quietly spoken bids or the quick slap of cards on the tabletop blended into the overall background sounds to which she had one ear attuned. She had hired a maid to come in and serve dessert and coffee, since it was her turn to entertain the group, and from the kitchen noises everything was on schedule.

Valerie played the hand at four hearts, found she had misjudged the placement of a king, but finessed her way to the contract. She was accepting her partner's congratulations and picking up her next hand when she felt a touch upon her shoulder. She turned to see Grace Bixby's smiling face. Grace was one of Valerie's oldest friends, but had been away on a three-week trip with her husband recently. "You look wonderful dear," Grace murmured in Valerie's ear as she sorted her cards. "Married life must really be agreeing with you."

Valerie flashed her a quick smile but said nothing.

Grace remained in her half-crouching position with her lips against Valerie's ear. "Do you see the brunette at table four? Facing us, with the long earrings? She's substituting, but she's been asking about you. Do you know her?"

Valerie looked at the smartly dressed woman whose features were strikingly handsome, then shook her head. "Should I?" she asked.

Grace shrugged as she straightened up. "Not as far as I know," she said, and returned to her table.

Two hands later Valerie found herself playing dummy, and left her table to check on things in the kitchen. Returning, she stopped and drew herself a half cup of coffee from the tall silver urn set up in the corner of the large room. She was joined almost at once by the striking-looking brunette from table four. "You don't know me, Mrs. Walker," the latter began, "but I couldn't refrain from having a word with you."

"Yes?" Valerie said cautiously.

"When I was asked to substitute today, I was about to refuse until I learned the address. Then my curiosity wouldn't permit me to stay away." Valerie remained silent, and the brunette glanced around the attractive room. "The house is still lovely."

"Still?" Valerie said before she thought.

The brunette smiled. "It probably wasn't protocol for me to come here today, Mrs. Walker, but I've already mentioned feminine curiosity. You see, I was your predecessor here. I was Mrs. Mark Walker, also. The second Mrs. Mark Walker, I might add."

Valerie felt a sense of shock. She tried to match herself to the calm of this woman who seemed very much in control of herself and the situation.

"How is Mark?" the brunette asked directly. They were standing far enough away from the bridge tables that their conversation could go unheard.

"Fine," Valerie said. "He's—fine."

The brunette shook her head. "A remarkable man. Remarkable." She smiled briefly with a flash of white teeth. "And the best I ever had in bed. But perhaps you've discovered that?" Valerie nodded numbly, then was furious at herself. Why should she respond at all to this probing?

The brunette was regarding her curiously. "Possibly you've found a way to hold him in check? You don't look the type for his usual accommodations. But then who should know better than I how clever he is at getting his own way?" She sighed and nodded at the chaise longue in front of the fireplace. "Would you believe that six months after I married Mark I held my younger sister down on that chaise while Mark raped her?"

A chill enveloped Valerie. Her throat felt dry, and she had difficulty in swallowing. Her companion seemed to expect no reply, however.

"It was when he began bringing girls in from the street that I walked out," the brunette continued. "After I could no longer supply him with accommodating girl friends any more. But if I know Mark, none of this is a surprise to you." She waited, but Valerie remained silent. The brunette gave a little laugh. "I'm a bitch, I know. Well, if it's any satisfaction to you—or to Mark either, for that matter— if I had it do over again I wouldn't walk out. I've missed too many good bedtimes in consequence. Good luck, Mrs. Walker."

The brunette returned to table number four, and Valerie walked to her own table. The import of what she had heard kept drumming at her consciousness. Nothing had changed; nothing would change. Except the natural events changed by time.

Valerie picked up her new hand and sorted cards blindly. She had already sat in her boudoir actually counting the days on her calendar until Neal and Ethel would be going away to college. They would be removed from Mark's influence, but Penny would still remain at home. And with the loss of stimulation caused by Neal's and Ethel's absence, would Mark become restless? Begin to look outside his home for stimulation? Valerie tried to hold down a rising tide of panic. Ethel and Neal would be home often on vacations, she consoled herself.

"Your bid, Val," her partner said impatiently.

"Uh—two diamonds," she responded.

She was forced to watch her partner play the hand at five clubs and go down three as a consequence of Valerie's unmotivated opening bid. The partner regarded her sourly.

But the hiatus gave Valerie time to think.

She looked across the room speculatively to Grace Bixby's table. Grace was blind as a bat without her glasses, and her nose was a bit too prominent, but she had a bright smile, a tall, full-bodied figure featuring a truly spectacular bosom, and good legs.

And she was Valerie's best friend.

Valerie glanced at the chaise longue in front of the fireplace. Could she, Valerie Walker, hold her best friend

151

Grace Bixby's shoulders down on the chaise while Mark fucked her?

Of course it would never come to that.

So it couldn't hurt to invite Grace over some evening, without her husband Ed, when the children were out of the house and there would just be Grace, Mark, and Valerie.

Valerie had learned that Mark tended to become especially active in bed with her when his imagination had something to feed upon.

And she knew what she had with Mark Walker, she appreciated it, and she wasn't about to lose it.

That was really the only thing that mattered.

THE END

2504707

Made in the USA